GRAND TOUR INTO DEATH

Roman Empire
in the second century AD

Under the reign of the Emperor Hadrian (117 – 138 AD), the power of the Roman Empire reaches to the borders of the known world. Even the most remote provinces enjoy unprecedented peace and prosperity.

Travel—by sea and land—is arduous and sometimes life-threatening, but the Roman elites are not deterred from taking on these hardships for the pure enjoyment of pleasure trips.

The cultivated Roman travels the classical sites of Greece and mysterious Egypt. He visits the famous temples and oracles, the legendary battlefields and the birthplaces of myths—but above all the *Septem Spectacula*: the greatest attractions of antiquity.

The Seven Wonders of the World.

I

I stood on deck and looked south, where the legendary Pharos would soon show us the way—the famed lighthouse of Alexandria.

Night had long since fallen. An infinite number of stars twinkled in the sky, and the dark waves of the *Mare Nostrum*, as the Romans proudly called it, pounded ceaselessly against the ship's hull.

Our sea. The Romans claimed it as a matter of course, just as they now called half the world their own. Even ancient and mysterious Egypt, where we would soon disembark, was now nothing more than a province on the southern border of the empire.

"Thanar!" A soft female voice called my name. I didn't have to turn around to know whose it was.

Layla.

She stepped out next to me at the ship's railing and put her hand on my arm. Her hair and skin, as dark as ebony, shimmered in the light of the lantern she carried.

Layla came from the fabled kingdom of Nubia, which lay south of Egypt, and she was an exquisite beauty. But what I loved even more about her was her gentle nature and razor-sharp mind.

No one could deceive or fool Layla. She was not a woman the average Roman would warm to—but after all, I wasn't the average Roman either. Actually, I was no Roman at all, but I belonged originally to the Germanic people who had settled beyond the northern border of the Empire.

However, for many years I had lived near the legionary base of Vindobona on the Danubius river, where I had made a name for myself as a merchant. And wicked tongues claimed that by now I had become more Roman than the Romans themselves.

I did not care for this criticism. I was certainly not a blind believer in Roman culture and lifestyle, but I am not afraid to confess that I have learned to appreciate the amenities of the Empire over these past years.

"No appetite, Thanar?" Layla said with a questioning smile. "Or else why did you leave us so early?"

She turned her head and cast a demonstrative glance over to the little group that had gathered at the back of the ship for dinner.

A short while ago I had sat with them and enjoyed the exquisite food, but immediately after the last bite I had gotten up to stretch my legs a little. In any case, I had put that forward as an excuse.

"Is the swell bothering you, master?" Layla asked me.

"Of course not," I replied quickly. "I'm fine. Everything is going well."

The fact that Neptune was once again restless in the depths of his ocean, throwing hard waves against the hull of our ship, did not bother me. And if it had, I would certainly not have admitted it to Layla, of all people.

For two weeks we had been at sea, and the crossing had sometimes been—well, let's say, adventurous.

But the imposing merchant ship that had taken us aboard held its own against the vagaries of the sea god. The freighter measured an incredible one hundred and thirty feet in length, could load up to twenty thousand bushels of grain, and had room for two hundred and fifty passengers. And the captain was a man of honor. Our chances of not being kidnapped at sea and sold into slavery were excellent. At least, that's what I hoped.

Layla addressing me as "master" was a mistake, or rather an old habit she sometimes still fell into. I had once been her master and she my slave. But that belonged to the past; in the meantime, she had become my freedwoman, no longer in my service, and I treated her as such.

Oh, what am I talking about! I treated her like a queen!

Layla's gaze met mine, and as always I had the impression that she could read everything she wanted to know in my eyes. Every single one of my thoughts. She was my black Sphinx, my sorceress—who had stolen my heart and clouded my senses. It was for her sake that I now stood here on board this ship, on my way to that city which was surpassed only by Rome itself in splendor and beauty: Alexandria.

I looked over at our traveling companions, who had just passed informally from dinner to a drinking bout. Laughter and the eager murmur of voices rose from the table.

We had been able to get hold of one of the coveted places on deck for the crossing to Alexandria, where we could sleep at night under the stars or in our tents, depending on the weather, and indulge in idleness under sun sails during the day.

The unfortunate passengers traveling in the hull of the ship had to put up with the heat and the confinement and the musty stench of bilge water.

Layla eyed me questioningly.

"So why are you standing here all alone at the railing, master? Instead of enjoying a good cup with your friends? It is our last night on board, after all."

She could really be persistent. And curious.

"I have no objection to a good cup of wine," I said. "You know that. But I can't stand the endless ramblings of that braggart anymore!"

She smiled knowingly. "You mean Capito?"

"Who else?" I shot back.

Even now, the voice of that creep could be heard loud and clear, although I had sought some distance from my friends. As on every evening, Capito did not miss the opportunity to entertain our traveling party with his worldly experience, his adventures, and his crazy stories. That's why I had sought the distance and foregone a good amphora of wine.

Layla's smile widened. She nodded her head in understanding.

"Yes, well, he sometimes overdoes it a little," she said. "I've never met a person who could talk so incessantly. But he is a very successful writer, isn't he? People seem to like his travelogues."

"Travelogues?" I exclaimed. "Please! I'd bet my right arm that not even half of them are true! The man is a consummate liar. And an impostor! He claims to have been everywhere! And his constant jokes, I really can't stand them anymore."

Capito loved the old Greek jokes about Elithios Phoitetes, which were usually heard at only very advanced hours, and in the most primitive pubs.

The name Elithios Phoitetes meant *idiot student* in Greek—and that said it all. One might have thought that Capito had been a fellow student of the man in question. The gods had truly not blessed him with too much intelligence.

Just now, the chatterbox was delivering another one of these jokes in a carrying voice:

"Elithios Phoitetes is traveling across the sea with his slaves on a ship. When a storm comes up and the slaves begin to howl that they will all die, he says to them: 'Stop howling, you wimps. In my will I have given you your freedom.'"

How exceedingly original....

During the dinner we had just eaten, Capito's tongue had hardly stopped for a moment. It was a wonder the guy hadn't starved to death at the table! Aside from the jokes already mentioned, Capito had shared a particularly hair-raising story tonight, about one of his supposed adventures.

As if in passing, he had told us about a sea voyage that had allegedly taken him far beyond the Pillars of Hercules, to the southern tip of Africa. Yes, he'd even claimed to have circumnavigated it! He'd said that the sun had been on his left. In the north!

And he'd also claimed to have met wild women, whose whole body was covered by thick black hair, during his over-land journeys. In the language of the natives, they were supposedly called *gorillas*.

What utter nonsense!

Layla seemed to be thinking about something.

Then she said, "I can't imagine that even half of his

stories are true."

A smile flitted across her face. "I'd say more like a tenth. At most."

We both had to laugh.

II

Gnaeus Saufeius Capito, as the braggart's full name was, claimed to have been in places I wasn't even convinced existed.

While we had been traveling the dusty roads between Ephesus and Halicarnassus, he had told us, for example, about his travels to the north. He'd said he'd reached Ultima Thule, the extreme northern edge of the world, which not even a Germanic traveler had ever reached.

On another of his foolhardy voyages, he'd claimed to have met dog-headed people and to have reached the Jade Gate in the farthest east. He'd asserted that he'd traveled on ships with purple sails and silver oars. Several times he had allegedly been kidnapped by pirates, but he had persuaded them by mere oratory to set him free again.

I could even imagine the latter. Presumably, after a few days of captivity, they had abandoned him on some island because they could no longer stand his incessant chatter.

Capito talked without stopping, speaking in such a carrying voice that he might have been on the stage of a theater. And he wrote just as eagerly, filling scroll after scroll with the adventures of his present journey. I could vividly imagine how he was embellishing his experiences and would later sell them for unseemly amounts of money to gullible Romans who had never gone further in their lives than the Italian hills.

At first, Capito's stories might have been exhilarating,

and some of the more soft-hearted members of our traveling party—Layla included—were still willing to listen to him. But in the meantime I avoided the man as much as possible.

I could see that now, as our traveling companions were indulging in the pleasures of Bacchus, he had taken a fancy to Alma. She had stretched out beside him, and her long golden-blonde hair fell in perfect waves over her shoulders. A beautiful sight, I had to admit.

Poor thing, went through my head. She was just too kind to turn away this chatterbox. Or to take flight, as I had done.

Alma's patience appeared to be inexhaustible. She seemed to be listening intently, while occasionally sipping from her wine cup. Every now and then she nodded her head, smiled at Capito, or made a graceful gesture with her slender arms.

Alma loved to listen to stories of wondrous journeys. She herself had hardly seen anything of the world yet. It was only since her husband's recent death that she had fulfilled a long-cherished dream and set off for distant shores. Our paths had crossed in Ephesus. We'd found that we had planned almost the same itinerary, and we had been traveling together ever since. Unfortunately, our way had also coincided with that of the chatty Capito.

Alma is really beautiful, went through my head. And she was also kind and gracious, even towards the charlatan driving me crazy with his unbearable chatter.

Alma Philonica was a widow from Rome, and still quite young. That is, originally she had come from the far north like myself. She often spoke of the endless forests and the wild ocean on whose shores she had spent her childhood. She seemed to have loved both very much, the forests as well as the ocean. She had never quite been able to get used to city life in Rome, where she had spent nearly the whole ten years of her marriage.

Her father, about whom she spoke little, had given her in marriage at the age of sixteen to a capable medicus who had later achieved social status and a handsome fortune in Rome. Alma did not seem to like to talk about her husband either.

What I had put together was that both men—the father and the spouse—had caused Alma much pain. When she spoke of her life, there was often talk of imprisonment and punishment, almost as if she had been a slave who had now finally gained freedom. And she seemed determined to enjoy her new life to the fullest.

Alma traveled with her body slave, a certain Zenobia, to whom she was devoted almost as a sister. She was also accompanied by a modest number of very capable servants and a handful of guards.

Alma had first set out from Rome to Ephesus to visit the world-famous Temple of Artemis. The *Artemision*, as most people called it, had also been the first stop on my journey with Layla.

Ephesus was located in a beautiful bay by the sea. It was a city thriving with life and sensual pleasures, and taverns, inns and stores lined the marble-paved streets. In the squares and markets one encountered courtesans with colorful fans, dressed in bright yellow, blue or purple robes, and with silver shoes on their feet. Merchants from Persia, Egypt and even more far-flung countries offered their wares for sale. Jugglers, dancers, and musicians outdid themselves with their arts, and the wine never stopped flowing.

The Artemision, however, was the crowning glory of all this splendor. It was said that the best builders of their time had taken a hundred and twenty years to erect the temple. In brilliant white it rose above the eternal blue of the ocean, and the greatest sculptors of Greece had vied for the honor of decorating the endless columned halls with their works of art.

Marble and gold delighted the eye wherever one turned. Fifty feet above our heads was the cedar roof structure, in itself a marvel of architecture—but the most imposing sight was the cult statue of the goddess herself.

Made of gold, stone and ebony, Artemis met her devotees with incomparable grace and power. She wore a skin-tight robe of the finest leather, the golden headdress of a queen, and was surrounded by her sacred creatures. The lion, the griffin, the bee, the deer....

None of us could get enough of the sight of it, and each acquired an artistic miniature replica of the unique statue before we continued our journey. I myself had also purchased a silver miniature of the temple for my art collection in distant Vindobona.

Both Alma and Layla worshiped the goddess Artemis in a special way, regarding the virgin huntress and mistress of moonlight as a role model and a patron. Artemis was wild and unruly, and her silver arrows never missed their target. Strong, proud and free as the wind, she roamed the woods with her nymphs, and no man ever succeeded in forcing his will upon her. The Romans called her Diana.

In the evenings in Ephesus, Layla and Alma had often sat together for hours of conversation, and became good friends. They both loved books, traveling, and the life stories of extraordinary women. One of their favorite subjects, the legendary Amazons, had been royal women who'd led tribes, gone to war, founded cities, and had defied even the greatest Greek heroes in the use of spear and bow.

We had met both Alma and Capito the chatterbox at the inn where we had lodged. At the end of our stay in Ephesus, we'd decided to continue our journey together. Because Capito and Alma had the same goal as we did: they wanted to see the *Septem Miracula*, the seven greatest sights of our world. Of which the Artemision had been only the first.

III

A trip to see the Wonders of the World—it was the dream of every educated Roman, and also one of Layla's greatest wishes. That was why I had suggested this journey to her.

I may not be a great warrior, like so many other men of my people, yet I had decided to fight for Layla.

Of course I was interested in the Wonders of the World, too, but the real purpose of this adventure with Layla was to snatch her from the arms of my friend and rival Marcellus.

He was young, brilliant, courageous, came from a distinguished Roman family, and by now held the title of legate. He had risen to become commander-in-chief of the Legio X Gemina, which was stationed in Vindobona, the town where I'd made my home.

Layla and I had met him in the midst of a terrible series of murders that had struck Vindobona. It was only thanks to Layla's cleverness that we'd been able to solve the bloody deeds in the end and bring the murderer to justice. Marcellus and I had been involved, but at best in a supporting role.

The relationship between Marcellus, Layla and me was complicated. As far as I knew—or rather hoped—Layla loved us both. Marcellus, the young, noble commander, and me, the somewhat aging barbarian whose slave she had once been. She was still part of my familia, as was the custom with many freed slaves. Layla had a permanent place in my house, but lately I had seen her far too seldom. She'd spent most of her time with Marcellus, in the legate's palace, where he'd showered her with almost foolish affection and expensive gifts.

Silk, furs, pearls ... these things certainly made an impression on Layla, but I could offer her what her heart really beat for: a tour of the world! Adventures in distant lands, which she'd known until now only from her books.

Marcellus was not only my competitor when it came to Layla; he was also one of my best friends. Yes, I loved him almost like a son. So I was plagued by remorse, in wanting to take his beloved away from him—but after all, he had taken her away from me, too. And in the end, he and Layla were not a good match. A Roman nobleman like him could never marry a freedwoman. I, on the other hand, could.

As I said, it was complicated.

The trip to the Wonders of the World was my last attempt to win Layla back to me. A whole year in cozy togetherness, far away from Marcellus, sharing adventures in the most spectacular places in the world. If that didn't help, then it was hopeless.

Some philosophers claimed that constant traveling—as was fashionable among certain rich Romans—did not solve any problems, because you always took yourself with you, no matter where you went. But I didn't put much stock in that.

I'd suggested the trip to the Wonders of the World to Layla, and she'd immediately been on fire for it.

As you can imagine, Legate Marcellus had been far less taken with the idea. He'd certainly seen through my plans, but he'd proved to be a generous opponent. He himself was, of course, indispensable to the legionary camp, but he'd given Layla a year for her journey with me. He had not wanted to, and could not, spare her any longer than that, as he'd said. His self-confidence was impressive. He seemed to have no doubt that she would find her way back into his arms when she returned home.

Well, my dear Marcellus: not if I had my way!

One year was not an overly generous time frame for such a long journey. We had to choose our route carefully. For weeks, Layla and I had pored over travel descriptions, road directories, and maps, making complicated calculations for the various modes of transportation available to us on each leg of our dream route.

In the end, it had come down to agreeing on six wonders of the world that we wanted to visit. There simply wasn't enough time to see all of them.

Scholars and philosophers did not have a unified list of what was considered a wonder of the world and what was not. One famous world traveler spoke of seven spectacula, another of nine, the next even of thirteen. And the opinions about what constituted a wonder of the world, and what was to be considered merely an outstanding sight, differed just as widely.

We decided to leave out one place that did appear on most lists: Babylon. The legendary royal city lay far to the east, away from the other spectacula that all lined up around the Mediterranean. And from all we had read, none of Babylon's once highly praised wonders remained.

The legendary tower, which the famous Herodotus had still seen with his own eyes, had already degenerated into a heap of rubble during the lifetime of Alexander the Great and in the meantime had completely disappeared from the face of the earth.

Of the massive fortress walls of the city, which seemed to have been built for eternity, only ruins were said to remain.

I would have loved to see this structure with my own eyes. I had trouble even imagining its vast dimensions. The walls were once over fifty miles long, two hundred feet high, flanked by towers that rose into the clouds, and so wide that two four-horse chariots could pass each other on the top of the wall!

Layla, on the other hand, had read with enthusiasm about the hanging gardens of Semiramis, also in Babylon. A traveler of our time could no longer see this former Wonder of the World with his own eyes either. A vertical garden, a blooming oasis high above the roofs of the city, it was said to have once been, watered by a true marvel of engineering.

This restriction on our plans had not seriously dampened Layla's enthusiasm, however. The remaining six showpieces were spectacle enough for us, and we also planned to visit countless other sights along our route: the dwellings and tombs of heroes and scholars, famous oracles, places of worship of the gods, battlefields, and magnificent temples with their precious art treasures.

IV

We'd set out in the month of Mars, just after the snow had melted.

The roads in the Imperium Romanum were passable even if you sank into the mud elsewhere; they spanned gorges and meandered boldly over mountain passes. Milestones and road signs, as well as the excellent maps with which we had equipped ourselves, always pointed us in the right direction. Only rarely did we go astray or take an unintended detour.

I'd had spacious and comfortable travel wagons made and gathered around me a handful of my most loyal servants and experienced guards. Street robbers were largely a thing of the past thanks to the tireless Roman patrols, but I preferred to play it safe.

In the course of our journey, we took up quarters in hostels, inns, roadhouses, and post stations. Some of these accommodations were rather modest, if not full of vermin, while others advertised comforts normally experienced only in the capital city. In towns and ports where I knew business associates, they readily granted us hospitality in their homes.

Our route first took us from Vindobona in the direction of Asia Minor. There, three wonders were on our sightseeing program: the Artemision in Ephesus, the Mausoleum of Halicarnassus, and the Colossus of Rhodos. The latter was already in ruins—it had been brought down by an earthquake four hundred years before our time, but even these imposing ruins were supposedly still worth a visit. At least, that's how they were described in the literature we had studied. And we were not to be disappointed when we finally reached the island of Rhodos.

The Colossus was the giant statue of Helios, the sun god and immortal owner of the island. Zeus himself had once given him the island as a gift, and the Rhodians had dedicated a glorious statue to him in the harbor of their city.

A hundred feet this statue had once reached into the sky. My traveling companions and I could testify to this, for we saw the huge bronze fragments with our own eyes.

A hundred feet! Made of bronze! Only the gods themselves knew how the sculptor—Chares of Lindos— had accomplished this miracle. The city guides, who forced themselves on us in the harbor, claimed that Helios in person had assisted the artist in melting and shaping the metal. We had no trouble believing this. A single finger of the statue was so thick that not even a giant of a man could embrace it with his arms.

Even the chatty Capito was speechless at the sight!

From Rhodos, the journey took us across the Mare Nostrum, the Mediterranean Ocean, which was by far the faster and less tedious route, compared to the overland one. We'd bought passage on the huge merchant ship on which we had been sailing across the sea for two weeks now.

In Egypt, which we would reach later tonight, we had two wonders of the world on our agenda: the Lighthouse of Alexandria and the Great Pyramids on the Nile.

Whether the pyramids were worth visiting was debatable—according to the great scholar Pliny, they were completely useless structures and not worth the trip. However, after all I had read from other famous writers, I certainly didn't want to miss them. And neither did Layla.

For Alexandria we had put together a very ambitious sightseeing program, and beyond that, other important sights in Egypt beckoned: the Canopus Canal with its sites of pleasure and vice, Heliopolis and Crocodilopolis, as well as Memphis and the Great Labyrinth.

On the way back, we again wanted to travel by ship across the Mediterranean and see the last of our selected miracula in Olympia: the statue of the divine Zeus, which was claimed to be more than just a work of art of the very highest order. It was said that the presence of the father of the gods in this cult image was palpable even to the most hopeless atheist. And I was certainly not a man who didn't honor the gods.

"Thanar?" A woman's voice brought me back to the present, one I would have recognized among thousands.

The diverse impressions of our journey so far, which had passed before my inner eye like a parade of images, faded and receded into the background.

I turned to Layla, who was still standing at my side. "I'm sorry ... what did you say?"

She gestured with her head toward our traveling companions. "I asked if you would like to come to Alma's aid. I'm sure she'd be grateful if you freed her from Capito's clutches. I'm afraid he'll talk both her ears off if you don't."

She grinned at me encouragingly. But I did not return

her smile.

"You think I don't realize what you're doing?" I burst out.

Layla looked at me, startled. "What do you mean, master?"

"Oh, please! Don't play the clueless one. You know exactly what I mean. You want to set me up with Alma—and you've been doing it since Ephesus! Do you think I'm so dumb that I don't notice that? And what is perhaps the more important question: do you really want to get rid of me so badly? Is my affection that troublesome to you?"

She said nothing in return. Only in her eyes I thought I perceived a great sadness.

"Do you miss Marcellus?" I asked her spontaneously.

She tilted her head. "Thanar, it's really not that—"

"Answer my question," I interrupted her briskly. "Do you miss him? Do you long to be back with him?"

She looked me straight in the eye. "I'm enjoying our trip, Thanar. Very much so. I don't want to be anywhere else. I'm very grateful to you for that."

"Grateful!" I snorted.

I didn't want her thanks, I wanted her love, damn it! But slowly I was coming to a point where I was no longer willing to humiliate myself for it. I had really done enough to reveal my feelings to her. Nothing, absolutely nothing, had I left undone in the last weeks and months to win back her heart. I was tired of it.

Was that perhaps because Alma had now entered my life? Of course I was annoyed about Layla's so obvious matchmaking. But was I possibly not so averse to turning my attention to the beautiful widow, if I was to be completely honest with myself?

25

Since we had boarded the cargo ship in Rhodos, I had repeatedly found myself having hour-long conversations with Alma, conversations that I enjoyed. Usually I only knew how to enjoy my time at Layla's side. Even when I merely stood next to the young widow at the railing and looked out to sea, I was content. No, more than that: filled with quiet joy. What more could a man ask for?

I spontaneously came to a decision. Layla wanted to set me up? Very well, she should have her way! I liked Alma, found her very attractive, felt comfortable in her company. I would not deny it from now on. Neither to myself, nor in front of Layla!

However, before I could come to the aid of our traveling companion—as Layla had suggested—and free her from the clutches of the rambling Capito, the passengers on deck suddenly got moving.

The jumble of voices grew loud. As one man, the people who had just been lying together over food and wine jumped up. From one moment to the next everyone was on their feet and pushing toward the railings.

"The lighthouse, it's over there!" The call resounded across the deck like a hundredfold echo.

And there it was, the Pharos, the world-famous lighthouse of Alexandria.

Only a tiny, still quite pale glow of light could be seen on the horizon. But soon we would be able to admire the Pharos at full size, and its beacon would turn night into day.

V

When our proud freighter finally entered the harbor, the light of the Pharos was so bright that it illuminated the entire quay.

You may be thinking: what could be so special about a lighthouse that it would be declared a wonder of the world? A justified objection, but while standing at the foot of this triumph of technology, such concerns were immediately swept aside.

An incredible four hundred feet high, the Pharos towered above us. You had to strain your neck to grasp its full size from the quay. At the same time, however, the structure was so slender that one might fear that the first storm would bring it down.

The beacon burned at every hour of the day and night and could be turned in any direction with the help of an ingenious mirror construction.

From the top of the tower, a huge bronze figure greeted the travelers. It was Alexander himself, the legendary founder of the city, even if the great man had never laid eyes upon the newly built metropolis before his death.

It took quite a while to unload our wagons, mounts, pack animals, supplies and luggage from the belly of the big freighter. Hours passed, which we used to take a close look at the famous lighthouse. It was only thanks to the bright light of the Pharos that the harbor was as bustling in the middle of the night as it might have been elsewhere at noon.

Layla and I had originally planned to stay in one of the many inns available to travelers in Alexandria. There were lodgings to suit every need—and every budget. But Gaius Brutus Faustinius, another of our traveling companions, had other plans for us.

Faustinius had joined us in Halicarnassus, the second stop on our Wonders of the World tour. Or rather, we had joined *him*. For the entourage with which he traveled resembled a small army, compared to which we and our modest servants hardly stood out. Faustinius was a millionaire, and he did not take a single step without the appropriate luxury and pomp.

Halicarnassus was the location of the world famous tomb of Mausolos, the tyrant—the Mausoleum. It was absent from practically none of the world wonder lists.

Mausolos had been nothing more than an insignificant provincial prince, hated by the people, but a visionary in terms of his dreams. He'd wanted his posthumous fame to be as great as that of any emperor, and so he'd gathered the most talented artists of his time around him and had asked them to build a tomb the likes of which the world had never seen. An imposing temple on a stepped foundation formed the base, above which rose a pyramid, and on this in turn was enthroned a quadriga of noble horses sculpted from the finest marble.

We'd been standing in front of the magnificent building, admiring the countless sculptures and reliefs that adorned it—gods, heroes, Amazons, Olympic athletes, daredevil charioteers—when we'd met Faustinius.

Faustinius was a friend I had not seen for many years.

No, friend was actually too much to say, because in truth I didn't know him very well. I had only met him once before, and that had been many years before. But on that occasion I had saved his life. That's probably why we both still remembered it as if it had been yesterday, and the danger we had escaped together had forged an unbreakable bond between us.

Faustinius traded in the beasts for which the amphitheaters of the Empire had a never-ending need. Lions, bears, wolves and every exotic animal imaginable—Faustinius captured them all, and in great numbers, and he delivered them reliably and always on time to wherever they were required. Some gladiator fights or similar spectacles devoured hundreds of these animals at a time.

It had been near Vindobona that I'd first met Faustinius. At that time, his business had still been in its infancy and he'd only been able to afford a small escort. So he'd been set upon by muggers, who probably would have cut his throat, had I not just been passing by—with a much stronger escort.

Together we'd managed to put the bandits to flight, and subsequently I'd offered the badly injured Faustinius the hospitality of my own house. My servants had nursed him until he recovered ... and at that time he'd sworn to me that one day he would show me the extent of his gratitude.

When I met him again many years later, at the foot of the mausoleum, he was a changed man. He had made a fortune, but I found him brooding, almost sinking into melancholy. The tomb had made him meditate on his own mortality—and on the fact that his life was empty and without love. I learned that Faustinius, much like me, had fallen in love with one of his slave girls. He had acted more decisively than I and had married her shortly thereafter, but she had died giving birth to their first son, the child following her soon after. And she had left behind a broken man.

"Now it only remains for me to wander restlessly through the world," Faustinius explained to me. "I want to enjoy its beauties at least for a short while. Perhaps I should also invest my fortune in a tomb that will make me immortal—what do you think, Thanar, old friend? We ought to be remembered, shouldn't we? I don't want to have lived for nothing."

Faustinius insisted that we all join his traveling party. Not only Layla and myself, but also Alma and Capito, who had been traveling with us since Ephesus.

None of us objected. Since then, we had been traveling like princes, dining on the finest delicacies, drinking wine that might have cost its weight in silver, and we had never set foot in a post station or inn again.

The host of slaves with whom Faustinius traveled set up a camp for us, every night anew, which would have been worthy of a Caesar. And I found to my delight that our company was able to cheer up the gloomy millionaire; soon he was no longer talking about death and loss, but seemed to be enjoying the trip to the fullest.

In Alexandria, one of Faustinius's business partners had promised him hospitality in his villa—an invitation that Faustinius extended to us without further ado. A few more people and a handful of servants to be accommodated and fed were of no consequence, he claimed. Besides, his business friend Petronius had mentioned that he would not be in Alexandria himself at the time of our arrival. He was a respected and very wealthy citizen of the metropolis, who also held several political offices and traveled almost constantly.

Petronius's house turned out to be a real palace in the best district of Alexandria. It was a two-story villa, built in the Roman style and standing near the sea. It was so large that one could easily get lost in the corridors, atria and innumerable halls.

Dead tired, I fell onto the soft bed in the room assigned to me. My traveling companions moved into luxurious chambers very close to me, while Faustinius had a suite of rooms at his disposal in another wing of the house.

I crawled under the covers, closed my eyes and listened to the thousand voices of the nocturnal city. And when I finally—many hours later, it seemed to me—sank into Morpheus's arms, I heard a terrible scream.

VI

It was a woman who was screaming—and very close to my chamber.

Layla?

Alma?

I almost fell out of bed, and at first found no orientation in the unfamiliar room. I had extinguished all the lamps for my night's rest. Only a little moonlight was falling into the room through a small window.

I fumbled for my robe, which I had thrown over the back of a chair before going to bed, and pulled it over my head. Then I wrapped my belt with the sax—my short sword—around my waist. When someone was screaming, there had to be danger!

Thus clothed and armed, I rushed out into the corridor.

Once again, a scream shattered the nightly silence. An agonizing, half-mad sound.

I hurried into the darkness, and thought I saw a faint glimmer of light further ahead. I reached a junction from which another corridor led off—and there, in front of the second door on the right, I discovered Zenobia, Alma's body slave, armed with a lamp. She was a Nubian like Layla and as good a servant as one could wish for. She usually slept in front of her mistress' tent or chamber, ready day and night to fulfill Alma's every wish.

Zenobia was by nature a very skittish creature, but now she seemed beside herself with fear. The hand in which she held the lamp was shaking uncontrollably, while with the other she was pounding on the door as if out of her mind.

"What is the matter with you, mistress?" she cried. "*Why don't you let me in?*"

Apparently the door was locked from the inside.

Alma's door! I'd only noticed that now. I'd still been quite drowsy before, but now I realized that it must have been the young widow who had screamed so fearfully. Zenobia had probably been the first to be roused from her sleep.

At that moment, I heard Alma's voice: "A demon!" she sobbed.

Her cry came through the wood of the door, muffled, but the panic that lay within was unmistakable. "Here on my bed. It wants to kill me!"

I courageously pushed Zenobia aside and threw myself against the door. Fortunately, it didn't seem to be made of too sturdy a wood. Nevertheless, I had to attack it repeatedly until it finally gave way, groaning under my onslaught.

My shoulder throbbed with pain as I snatched the lamp from Zenobia's hand and entered the chamber. I quickly looked around.

In the room, only a tiny oil light burned on the bedside table. Its glow was lost in the spacious chamber.

I recognized Alma, who was huddled at the head of the bed. She had her arms wrapped around her knees and was pressing them tightly against her body.

When I approached her, her eyes widened in terror and fixed on me. She looked at me as if I were the great

Hercules himself coming to save her.

She released her right hand from her knees and pointed tremulously to the foot end of the bed.

"Demon," she breathed in a sepulchral voice.

I ran toward her and fixed my eyes on the spot she had pointed out. Only when I stood directly in front of it did an outline emerge from the shadows and I could see what was causing Alma such fear.

She had not exaggerated, it was indeed a hideous creature. A hairy, eight-legged monster, as big as the palm of my hand. Not a demon though, but a spider!

A demon in the form of a spider? I had never seen such a huge, disgustingly hairy specimen in my life.

When I took another step closer, the monster started to move. On its thin legs it was incredibly fast—and it ran right in Alma's direction!

This was not supposed to happen! My hand was already on the handle of my sax, which I was wearing on my belt. I had no time to hesitate. If I wanted to kill the beast before it reached Alma, I had to act right now, before I ended up hitting Alma's legs.

I leapt forward, blade drawn, aimed—and landed a hit! Thank the gods! I impaled the hairy monster with the blade and fixed it on the mattress, like a crucified villain.

Alma jumped out of bed and ran towards me.

"Oh, Thanar, thank you! Thank you!"

She wrapped her arms around my neck and pressed against me so hard that I almost lost my balance. I must admit that I was filled with pride. With pride and a very warm feeling in my heart when she nestled against me so passionately.

But I was not granted to savor this joyful moment for long. First Zenobia rushed to throw herself at her mistress' feet, sobbing with relief. Immediately behind her, a bony figure hurried into the room, a tall, lean man with deep-set, almost black eyes. He looked sleepy, was unarmed, and anyway he'd come much too late!

It was Timotheos, the scribe—or rather, private secretary—of Faustinius.

I must confess that I had no great sympathy for this fellow. I was of the firm opinion that my old friend Faustinius placed too much trust in the man, giving him too much responsibility and say in his business.

But that was ultimately no concern of mine. What bothered me much more was the way Timotheos—practically without interruption—fawned over Alma. Ever since Faustinius had joined us with his retinue of servants and slaves, Timotheos had been courting Alma. On board the ship that had brought us to Alexandria, it had become so conspicuous that the fellow had aroused my displeasure. If I'm honest, I would have loved to feed him to the fish. He was almost worse than Capito, the chatterbox!

Not for the first time, I had to think of the love-wisdom of the great Ovid. He'd advised women who wanted to win a man's heart to rely on the power of jealousy.

Had Alma studied the writings of the famous scholar? Had she let herself be courted by Timotheos, this scribbler, to make me jealous? If so, it had worked frighteningly well.

I had studied Ovid's famous *Ars amatoria*, his *Art of Love*, before Layla and I had left home in the spring. I'd wanted to prepare myself as thoroughly as possible. After all, our trip wasn't just about seeing the wonders of the world. I was going far away to win back Layla's heart.

I'd found some of the great scholar's advice rather strange, but he was probably right about jealousy. I didn't like the way this Timotheos was wooing Alma like a lovesick rooster.

Capito, the chatterbox, was also fond of laying siege to the beautiful widow, but as far as I could see, he did not dare make any amorous advances. He probably loved no one but himself, was so full of his own magnificence that he was blind and deaf to Alma's loveliness.

Now Timotheos stepped up next to me and spoke to Alma.

"By all the gods, what happened here?" he demanded to know.

Then he saw the impaled monster on Alma's bed. Startled, he backed away, but in the next moment he had already regained his composure. He probably didn't want to look like a coward in front of his adored one.

She released herself from my arms as if in a trance and turned to Timotheos, explaining.

"Thanar saved me," she said, and again my heart swelled with pride. I am an old, sentimental fool.

Timotheos gave me a hostile look. He probably would have preferred to play the hero for Alma himself.

Well, too late, my good fellow, I thought to myself, not without satisfaction.

Behind us, more servants pushed into the room. Zenobia, however, did not allow anyone near Alma. The dark-skinned slave protectively put her arm around her mistress like a mother and stared at the spider with her eyes widened in terror. "Oh, this horrible country!" she cried with fervor. "We should not have come here! All the evil omens on the journey ... now the gods are angry with us because we've disregarded all their warnings!"

Alma's servants were a frightened bunch who—just like Alma herself—had never traveled. They saw evil signs at every corner, and every single one of them seemed to be counting the days until they would be allowed to return to their familiar home. Zenobia was perhaps the most fearful of them all; with every new day, every visit, every bite of bread in a new tavern, she seemed to fear for Alma's life.

"Why don't you get your mistress a cup of warm wine," Timotheos interjected. "I'm sure it will do her good. Calm her mind."

I didn't like it at all that Timotheos was acting as Alma's protector. But before I could do anything, a soft rustling distracted me.

VII

As I was about to get to the bottom of the noise, Layla appeared next to me. She was wearing a tunic made of a shiny and gauzy fabric that clung to her body and must have caused the strange rustling. Layla looked like the goddess of the night herself in it.

Probably a gift from Marcellus, went through my head. My resentment grew. Was I doomed to always be placed second in the favor of women?

However, I did not allow myself any further thoughts on this unpleasant subject. Now was really not the place or time for jealousies. I told Layla—who looked at me questioningly—about what had happened in Alma's room. Then I pointed again with my hand to the beast I had killed.

Without hesitation Layla stepped closer to the bed and looked at the impaled carcass.

"A tarantula," she said after a few moments.

Her words sounded as casual as if she had merely inspected common vermin. But even as she spoke, her eyes wandered to the windows.

There were two double arched windows in the room, both glazed. In the warm climate of Alexandria, this was probably not necessary. Presumably, the owner of the house had ordered the expensive glass inserted only to show that he could afford it.

"I wonder how the spider got in," I heard Layla mutter.

"Not through the window, anyway."

"Actually a spider?" I repeated. I concealed from Layla that Alma had mistaken the animal for a demon and had suffered mortal fears. In the deserts of Egypt, which was a land of sorcerers and necromancers, the darkest powers dwelled. Every child knew that. But a spider as big as a plate? How could there be such a thing?

"Would she have killed me?" I heard Alma say. Her warm green-brown eyes were fixed on Layla. "If Thanar hadn't rushed to my rescue?"

Layla shook her head. "The bite of a tarantula is painful, for sure, but its venom is only weak. It can't harm a human."

At that moment Zenobia returned with a silver tray on which she carried a wine cup for Alma. She led her mistress to one of the comfortable chairs that stood under the windows and poured her the warm drink.

Layla, meanwhile, picked up the tray that Zenobia had set down, walked over to the bed, and unabashedly grabbed the dead monster. She dropped it on the tray, and wordlessly returned my sax to me.

"I'd better take this critter away," she said. "It's not a pretty sight."

That was Layla at her best. Courageous, unshakable, and able to cope with any event, no matter how strange.

I breathed a sigh of relief. If Layla was right about the spider—which I didn't doubt—Alma had not been in any danger. Well, she had suffered a nasty fright and would perhaps dream of hairy giant spiders for a while, but that was still better than a demon in the flesh who wanted to kill her.

The gathering in Alma's room gradually dispersed. The slaves scurried away, back to their night's lodging. Only Zenobia stayed by her mistress' side, although Alma tried to send her away several times.

"Stop coddling me already, as if I were an infant," Alma scolded the woman, albeit with great tenderness in her voice. "You heard what Layla said. It was just a spider."

Alma had put on a brave face, but she did not completely convince me with it. The monster spider had given her a good scare. Just like me.

Layla finally escorted Timotheos from the room, for which I was very grateful to her.

"Alma needs her sleep now," she announced, sounding almost like Zenobia for a moment. Then she signaled to me with a nod that it was time for us to go, too.

When I said goodbye to Alma, she gave me a tender look, and I told myself that she would have gladly put up with my company for a while longer.

Anyway, Layla knew how to redirect my thoughts quickly and mercilessly to another topic. To my surprise, she followed me into my bedroom—but without amorous motives, as I immediately discovered.

"We need to talk, Thanar," she said, right after she had closed the door behind us. "This spider—I don't like it at all."

I looked at her uncomprehendingly. "You just said she was harmless, or did I misunderstand? So why are you worried? And how do you even know about such monsters? What did you call her—a tarantula?"

"These critters also exist in my home country," Layla explained. "As a child, I was scared half to death when one of them entered our house."

"Scare *you* to death?" I joked, "I can't imagine that for the life of me. Not even the Lord of the Underworld himself could achieve that!"

Layla gave me a smile, but the next moment she became serious again. "The question is: how did this spider get into Alma's room? These animals can get into a cellar or a small house, but into a palace like this one? It couldn't have come through the windows, they're sealed with glass. And the masonry in this house is as solid as a fortress. No cracks or crevices, just fresh, perfect plaster everywhere. Mosaics or the finest stone on the floors. So how did the beast get into Alma's room? Are we to believe it crawled through the entire house? Up the stairs, down the hall? Past the eyes of dozens of servants and slaves?"

Now I understood what Layla was getting at.

"You think someone *planted* that beast in Alma's room?" I exclaimed. "On purpose? To scare her?"

"Maybe more than that," Layla replied. "*I* for one know that these spiders are harmless. But that may not be true of others of our traveling companions. They might see the fearsome exterior—and think of a deadly demon. Perhaps someone believed they could poison Alma with the help of this animal."

"Oh, please, Layla, this is going too far," I protested. "You're not suggesting that someone wanted to kill Alma, are you?"

She looked at me seriously with her wise eyes.

"Would it be so inconceivable? Think back, master," she said. "Haven't we witnessed strange events several times on this journey already? Was it really the first incident that could have been an attempt on Alma's life? And as for the dark signs of the gods that have been haunting us since Ephesus...."

"Oh, please, Layla, don't you start with that too! You're not a superstitious little slave anymore. What am I talking about—you've never been one! Dark signs, my ass! You're just saying that to make me worry about Alma, admit it! You want to convince me that she needs protection, so that I devote myself to her, stay near her...."

Layla shook her head vigorously.

"That's not true. Not this time, master. I admit that I would like her to be my friend. And also, that I would want to see her at your side. It would be so fitting, I think...."

She interrupted herself—probably because she noticed my ill-tempered look.

"No, honestly Thanar. I'm actually worried about her. You may not be frightened by the dark omens. You are a brave man in the face of any danger. I know that. But that does not mean we should throw the signs of the gods to the wind. Perhaps they were a warning."

"A warning about what?" I brashly interrupted her.

"Maybe about the very danger Alma might be in. Not necessarily from the immortals, but rather from an earthly adversary."

I reached for Layla's hands, gently taking them in mine.

"Honey, you can't smell foul play behind every corner!" I implored her, "even though I know how much you like being an, ahem, puzzle solver."

Layla was fond of travel and books and—maybe a little bit—of me. But she *loved* crime, especially murder, more than anything else. That might sound horrible, but it was still the truth.

Already twice Layla and I had been involved in terrible bloody deeds, within just a few months. First, a gruesome series of murders had shaken our hometown of Vindobona, and the second time death had even moved into my own house.

Had we really incurred the wrath of the gods, for them to be afflicting us in this way? And should it now be happening a third time? When we were nothing more than peaceful tourists?

Was death traveling with us, unrecognized in our midst, on our so very peaceful journey to the Wonders of the World? It was a terrifying thought.

Unfortunately, Layla was not entirely wrong about the dark omens she had mentioned. The signs had been unmistakable and numerous. Even if I had stubbornly refused to acknowledge them until now.

It had already started at the temple of Artemis. There a goat, the sacrificial animal we had chosen for the goddess, had not gone willingly to the altar, but had almost escaped.

Then, on the onward journey, a wheel on one of the travel wagons had broken twice in succession. Several times black ravens had flown over our heads in an ominous direction.

Just before we reached Halicarnassus, we'd suddenly heard the howling of dogs outside the inn where we were spending the night—an omen that heralded an imminent death.

When we had boarded the ship in Rhodos that was to take us to Alexandria, one of Alma's slaves had sneezed. I think it was Zenobia—just as she had walked the plank onto the ship. The captain almost didn't take us with him, even though Faustinius had already paid him handsomely. Shortly thereafter, Capito had discovered a crow in the ship's rigging.

I could only vaguely remember a whole series of other small incidents. Which unfortunately did not mean that they could be ignored.

"Nevertheless," I said to Layla, "we should not overestimate these signs. They may herald disaster ... but that doesn't mean any of us are in mortal danger. And not Alma, of all people."

Layla examined me from her large dark eyes. "And that roof tile in Rhodos? What about it? Do you think that was just an accident?"

VIII

"Of course I think so!" I burst out. "What else could it have been? The tile was just loose and fell off the roof. That's really not a rare occurrence."

In Rhodos, the third stop on our Wonders of the World route, we had visited the famous Colossus. Or rather the remains of it. I have already reported about this.

Quite a number of our slaves had loudly moaned and clamored about the fact that we wanted to visit Rhodos at all. In their opinion, a stay on an island where the patron god had toppled his own statue could only bring death and ruin.

Of course, we had not let ourselves be distracted by this chatter or even thought of changing our route.

On our last evening in Rhodos, however, we had been strolling through one of the alleys near the harbor when suddenly the aforementioned roof tile had crashed to the ground very close to us. It would not have taken much for it to have buried Alma under it.

Layla regarded me with a furrowed brow. "I didn't mention it that night," she said hesitantly, "because I didn't want to worry you. And because I wasn't really sure exactly what I had seen."

"What you had seen?" I repeated. "Well, what did you see, Layla? Don't talk in riddles like that!"

She hesitated again, but then she said, "A shadow, Thanar. Above our heads. On that roof from which the tile fell. But as I said, it was dark, I could not be sure. Maybe it wasn't an assassin, but just an animal going its way."

"But now you think that this shadow was trying to kill Alma? And that tonight, with the help of the monster spider, he made a second attempt—not knowing that this vermin is not as deadly as it looks? Is that what you wanted to say?"

Layla tilted her head. "I'm just saying that you ... that *we* ... should keep an eye on Alma, that's all. It was just the three of us that night in Rhodos, remember? Alma, you and I. You even gave our guards the all clear because we weren't in any danger in the city. So anyone from our group could have followed us and sneaked onto the roof. And then...."

"Enough," I snapped.

Reluctantly, I shook my head, as if I could thus dispel the gloomy thoughts Layla had just fed to me.

Of course it didn't help. Layla had achieved what she had intended—whatever motive might actually have been behind her words: genuine concern for Alma or just another attempt to win me over to the side of the beautiful widow. Or rather, to set me up with her.

In any case, I was now worried about Alma. The idea that something could happen to her was unbearable to me.

Layla, however, was far from ready to let it go: "Before, in Halicarnassus, towards the end of our stay there ... Zenobia was affected by that strange nausea. Do you remember?"

I gave her a somber look. "No, I guess I didn't notice any of that. What about it?"

"Well, she ate a sweet date dish—that her mistress had

left for her. Immediately after that, she became ill. Quite suddenly and quite violently. She threw up several times. But dates are actually palatable and digestible. And they also do not spoil easily at all."

Once again, I realized that Layla had a very different view of the world than I did. She seemed really determined to smell danger and conspiracy everywhere, while I went through the day in a much more carefree fashion.

"So you think this date dish was ... what, exactly? Poisoned? And that it was actually meant for Alma?"

"It's possible, isn't it?" Layla replied.

In Halicarnassus, as I mentioned earlier, we had encountered Faustinius and soon joined his traveling party. From then on, we'd no longer stayed in inns or post stations as before, but were guests in his luxurious camp. Which meant that his cook had prepared all the meals for us. Thus also the said date dish....

I lost myself in thought.

A misfortune that had already befallen us in Ephesus came to mind. Layla didn't know anything about it yet, because she hadn't been present on that occasion. Only I, one of my guards, and Alma and her faithful Zenobia had been out that evening.

My lad had been lighting the way with his lantern when suddenly, seemingly out of nowhere, a two-horse wagon had come hurtling around the corner of a house.

If Zenobia had not reacted so courageously and risked her own neck, Alma would have been run over. The brave slave had jumped in front of her mistress and had been able to push her aside in time. The charioteer had driven on at breakneck speed, as if he hadn't even noticed us.

I yelled a curse after the man—but that this almost fatal accident could have been a targeted attempt on Alma's life—well, the idea had not occurred to me. Now, however, it suddenly looked different, all thanks to Layla.

As I've said, I generally went through life optimistically. I trusted in the good in people—and that the gods were well-disposed toward us. Was I simply being naive? Reckless, even? Did Layla have a much more realistic view of things?

Had this supposed accident in truth also been an attempt on Alma's life?

Before I could ponder these questions further, there was a knock at the door of my chamber. Quietly and carefully—it sounded like a servant who was very reluctant to disturb me at such a late hour. But what had led him to me now?

A strange restlessness seized me. Had something else happened? Had some evil befallen Alma because I had left her alone—thinking she was safe?

IX

I jumped up, crossed the room quickly to the door and opened it.

In the doorway stood Optimus, one of the guards Marcellus had given Layla and me for the trip. The legate had insisted on reinforcing our security team with a few trusted men he knew.

Optimus had been with us since Vindobona and had proven to be a reliable and very capable guard. He was a veteran of the legion, who had recently completed his years of service.

Normally, soldiers like him would retire to a nice piece of land, but Optimus was not cut out for a life of idleness. He had made that clear to me right at the beginning of our trip.

As a matter of course, he had taken over the leadership and allocation of the guards who accompanied us on the journey. The other men had soon recognized his authority just as naturally.

Optimus was a powerfully built fellow, with a weather-beaten face and arms like tree trunks. The mere sight of him had already scared off many a sinister fellow who might otherwise have seen tourists like us as uninformed and easy victims.

At the beginning of our journey, before we'd met Faustinius, we had sometimes had to seek shelter in very dubious hostels. In the larger cities, with a well-filled purse, one could find safe and comfortable quarters for the night, but in the countryside this was often not the case. Many a simple stable that advertised hospitality to travelers suddenly turned out to be a robber's nest.

In these places, Optimus had always made sure that we remained unmolested. No mugger or other dubious fellow, who valued his life, wanted to mess with the former soldier.

I had already made the resolution in Halicarnassus to offer Optimus a permanent position upon our return to Vindobona. He would make an excellent leader of my guards—the band of men I employed to ensure the safe conduct of my trade transports.

Now, however, Optimus looked worried. He started to speak as soon as I opened the door.

But when he caught sight of Layla, he interrupted himself.

"Excuse me, Thanar, you still have a visitor," he said in a reverent tone. "May I come back later? Or better tomorrow morning?"

"Speak up! Has something happened?" I asked with concern, but he assured me that everything was in order.

"There's just something I want to discuss with you, sir," he said.

At this late hour, went through my head.

Layla rose from the bench where she had made herself comfortable.

"Come on in, Optimus," she said, "I was just going to leave anyway. It's getting late."

She yawned demonstratively, wished me a good night and slipped out of the room.

I hadn't talked to her about it yet, but I was sure she thought as highly of our legionary veteran as I did.

Optimus stood hesitantly at the threshold and looked after Layla as she disappeared silently into the corridor. He was probably a little unsure as to whether he had driven her away with his appearance. Perhaps he also wondered what had brought her to my room at such a late hour.

As a soldier who until recently had been under Marcellus's command, he was well aware that Layla was the legate's mistress.

However, in the months that we had been traveling together it couldn't have escaped Optimus how I felt about Layla. He was an attentive observer who hardly missed anything, yet he also knew how to look away discreetly when it seemed necessary.

I didn't know what Optimus thought of the strange love triangle between Marcellus, Layla, and me, but I wasn't going to discuss the matter with him. The legate certainly hadn't either.

With a nod of my head, I told the veteran to finally come in. I realized that I was very sleepy by now, but if Optimus had come to see me at such a late hour, he must have something urgent on his mind.

I directed him to take a seat, but he preferred to remain standing.

Of course, what did I expect? Optimus believed himself to be on duty at all hours. And he showed me respect as if I held the same rank as Marcellus, his former legate.

He hesitated before telling me his request—which was uncharacteristic for him. Normally, he spoke the way he moved: succinctly, with purpose, and at a brisk pace.

"Go ahead and tell me, Optimus," I prompted him. "What's on your mind?"

Finally, he took heart. "I have made an observation— which I wanted to report to you. It's about the incident in Alma Philonica's chamber. About the spider," he added, raising his eyebrows.

Most legionaries got around quite a bit in the world during their years of service. But a spider monster like the one in Alma's room didn't seem to be an everyday sight, even for Optimus.

Only now did I notice that Optimus had not been there when Alma had screamed and I had broken down the door to her room. That was also uncharacteristic for him. As I have already indicated, he took his position very seriously—and never seemed to close an eye. Had he thought us to be safe here in Petronius's palace and finally allowed himself some well-deserved rest?

I was wide awake again in one fell swoop. "Yes? What did you observe?" I asked him. "Out with it."

He nodded his head, barely noticeably. "I positioned myself for tonight's vigil, sir, so that I could keep an eye on more than just your chamber and Layla's. I chose a place farther forward, where the two corridors intersect, so that I could also watch the way to Alma's room."

"Why is that?" I asked him.

Well-deserved rest, my ass. Apparently, he had once again planned on burning the midnight oil.

I looked suspiciously into his face. Hopefully he would not now also approach me with the suspicion that Alma could be in danger? Layla's dark omens, strange accidents and other hints of menace had truly been enough for me.

He hesitated for a tiny moment.

"Well," he then said, "forgive me for being so blunt about it: it has not escaped me how much Alma means to you. So I consider it my duty to see to her safety as well."

"Ah yes," I muttered.

I couldn't think of anything wittier at the moment. Apparently, everyone around me seemed to know that Alma and I were meant to be together. Except I myself.

"Then where were you when Alma screamed—because she thought she was in mortal danger?" I asked him. "Why didn't you rush to her aid?"

He lowered his head guiltily. "I had just gone to the latrine, sir. And after that I ran to the servants' quarters to get something to eat. It was only when I returned that I learned from some of the slaves what had happened. And I was able to inspect the arachnid that you'd killed. I deeply regret my failure, sir. It was irresponsible. But I thought this house was well guarded, and hunger plagued me, because today I have not even—"

I raised my hand and interrupted him.

"You really don't have to apologize, my faithful Optimus. I see you awake and never sleeping or eating, at almost every hour of the day and night. You are really not to blame!"

He smiled gratefully and I asked him to finally come out with his request.

He cleared his throat.

"Of course, I don't want to raise any suspicions that I can't back up with solid evidence," he began, "and certainly, this peculiar arachnid may have found its way

53

into Alma's chamber all by itself...."

He broke off.

"But?" I asked. "You don't have to go easy on me, my dear Optimus. Do you have another explanation?"

I spoke the words lightly, but braced myself in my mind for what he was about to tell me. That Layla—as always—had not been mistaken, and someone was actually trying to kill Alma?

"It's just an observation I made, as I said," he continued. "And which I wish to report to you. It's about Lurco, sir. I saw him in the corridor outside Alma's room after you had all gone to sleep. This was quite a while before the incident with the spider, but he ... well, he was acting extremely strangely."

Lurco was the barber of Faustinius.

That is, originally he had probably filled this role. In the meantime, he was much more, almost a kind of body servant. And perhaps he also sweetened one or another of his master's nights as a lover boy, when Faustinius was tired of his slave girls and was looking for a change from feminine charms.

Lurco was the archetypal luxury slave, young and beautiful as a girl. Not a single hair could be seen on his arms or legs; indeed, his entire body was probably smooth and always groomed with expensive oil. He wore his hair shoulder-length, and the robes in which he used to wrap himself must have cost Faustinius a small fortune.

Moreover, Lurco was always in a good mood, knew how to listen and entertain his master with all kinds of jokes. He shaved him almost every day, and Faustinius also attached the greatest importance to a perfectly fitting hairstyle.

"I saw Lurco skulking in the hallway," Optimus repeated. "And he was carrying a knife in his hands. His gaze was fixed, as if he were possessed by a demon!"

X

This portrayal Optimus had given of Lurco was very much out of character for the playful boy-toy barber.

"He was carrying a knife?" I repeated. "There's nothing unusual about that—for somebody who's always cutting beards and hair, is there?"

Optimus grimaced. "He was certainly not on duty, sir. Neither was he coming out of Faustinius' rooms when I saw him, nor was he on his way there. Faustinius and his retinue are housed in another wing of the villa."

"I'm aware of that," I said.

"And if Faustinius had called his barber to him at this late hour ... then surely it was not for a shave," he added in a tactful tone.

I knew what he was getting at. You don't take a knife with you for a little love tryst with your master.

"Also, he wasn't carrying a shaving knife," Optimus continued. "It was dark in the hallway, but I know my way around blades pretty well, if I might add."

"Did you see if Lurco approached Alma's room?" I asked.

He shook his head. "Not when I saw him in the hallway. He might have crept up on her later, though. When I left my post."

Optimus lowered his eyes. Apparently, he was still castigating himself for what he saw as a terrible neglect of his duties.

"He could have been with Alma just before she

discovered the spider and screamed," he added.

I shook my head. "He was armed with a knife—and then supposedly smuggled a spider into Alma's room?" I said. "That makes little sense, if you ask me."

"That's true. As I said, I just wanted to report the incident, precisely because it seemed so strange to me. I asked Lurco where he was going with the knife. But he simply walked past me—it was as if he hadn't noticed me at all. I let him go, because at that time I had no idea that Alma would later ... that someone might want to harm her," he corrected himself.

He looked at me and pulled up his massive shoulders. "The decision, of course, is entirely yours, sir, whether you wish to pursue the matter."

I thought about it for a moment.

Then I turned to Optimus again: "Did you notice anyone else near Alma's room in the early hours of the night? If, as you said, you were keeping an eye on the door to her chamber."

"I saw no one who would have been out of place there," Optimus replied. "Zenobia came and went, of course, and once Layla did as well ... then a few servants of this house who brought food and drink and fresh water. But I saw no one else."

I made a decision without further ado. "See if you can find Lurco and bring him to me. If he's already asleep, wake him up."

Optimus nodded and was already about to turn on his heel to hurry out of the room.

"Wait," I held him back. "If Lurco should be with Faustinius, we'd better postpone the questioning until tomorrow. After all, in a way we are Faustinius's guests. I therefore do not wish to disturb his night's rest."

Even if Faustinius, should Lurco really be with him right now, probably didn't want to sleep. But I kept this thought to myself; my friend owed no one an account of his nocturnal pleasures.

I only had to wait a short while before Optimus returned. Next to him walked Lurco, who looked as light-footed as a fawn at the soldier's side.

The young barber was wrapped in a fine white silk tunic and literally floated over the floor. Apart from that, however, he seemed rather intimidated by the veteran of the legion. The subtle smile that usually played around Lurco's lips was gone.

"You wanted to see me, sir?" he asked uncertainly as he stepped in front of me.

I didn't beat around the bush.

"You have been noticed, tonight," I said to him, "in the hallway, close to here. Far from your master's chambers or the servants' quarters. Tell me, what were you up to?"

I deliberately didn't mention Alma, and did not accuse him of having anything to do with the spider in her room either. Undoubtedly the incident must have reached his ears, because such news spread faster than wildfire among the servants. But I did not want to accuse him right away; first I wanted to hear what he had to say in his defense.

He seemed—or rather pretended to be—clueless. "In the hallway? Me? Tonight? You must be mistaken, sir. I went to bed very early. The floor has been swaying under my feet since we disembarked the ship, and I have been feeling quite wretched."

Lurco was a pampered fellow—which was not surprising for a luxury slave. I could readily believe that he was not a great sailor and was still suffering from the after-effects of our ship's passage. Already on board I had often observed him emptying the contents of his stomach over the railing.

But he was obviously lying to my face. I would have expected him to present me with an excuse as to what he had been doing in our part of the house in the middle of the night. The fact that he simply denied having been here at all bordered on impudence. He must have seen Optimus, too, if the veteran had even spoken to him.

I glanced discreetly at Optimus, who had taken up position against the wall next to the door. Was he really sure that he had seen Lurco? Couldn't he have mistaken him for someone else?

Optimus seemed to be able to read my thoughts. In any case, he nodded at me resolutely.

I believed him. After all, Lurco didn't look like any other slave. His appearance, his mannerisms, the way he moved around—it was hard to confuse him.

I got up from my chair.

Lurco took a step back. "Sir?" he asked in alarm.

I tapped his chest with my finger and put on a scowl.

"I don't like being lied to," I said. "But maybe you just forgot where you went. Because you felt so wretched, as you say. So now I ask you again. What were you doing in the hallway? You were seen, Lurco. With a knife in your hands!"

The young barber shook his head vigorously. "A knife?

59

No, sir, I swear it. I—"

"Enough," I exclaimed, silencing the fellow with a wave of my hand.

Lurco looked around as if he were pursued, then he squinted his girlish eyes and whispered, "It must have been a haunting that dulled your senses, sir! It was not I whom you saw, but a dark sorcerer. Little wonder, in this land of sorcerers and necromancers, of the living dead! Oh, how I have begged our master not to travel to this accursed land. We'll all end up being devoured by demons!"

With these words he turned and rushed out of the room.

Optimus jumped after him, trying to grab him, but I called him back.

"Leave him, my good man! We'll sort it out tomorrow. I'm dog-tired, and I'm already sick of this superstitious chatter. Demons, sorcerers, necromancers...."

I groaned and rubbed my heavy eyelids. "Enough of this nonsense! For tonight, anyway."

For a large number of the servants who accompanied us, Egypt was the forecourt of the underworld. The country was thousands of years old and terrified people with its strange customs, magical script, and especially its cult of the dead.

"I will see if I can talk to Faustinius about this tomorrow," I said to Optimus. "For tonight, I'm going to lock my door and go to sleep. And you should do the same. Give yourself a break, Optimus. I don't think we're in any serious danger in this house. I don't know why Lurco would lie to us, but I can't imagine him as a treacherous assassin either—not by any stretch of the imagination. Maybe there is a harmless explanation for everything. And that spider may just have gotten lost."

Yes, I wanted to believe that.

But I was to lie sleepless in bed for a long time, pondering eight-legged vermin, and whether Layla's gloomy view of things was—once again—the right one. Were the gods about to afflict us anew with death and destruction?

XI

When I went to check on Alma the next morning, I found an older slave woman in the room with her. She introduced herself to me as Veronica, the head of Petronius's house slaves, and was about to apologize to Alma in an almost tearful tone.

"I can't explain how the spider got into your room," she sniffed as she bowed incessantly to Alma while pounding her fist against her own chest. "These creatures are found all over Alexandria, in the gardens, in the cellars—but not once has one entered this house. We keep our master's mansion free of all vermin. Never yet have we failed in this!"

She acted like a commander throwing himself at his Caesar's feet because he had made a fatal mistake, one which had cost him one or two of his cohorts. The woman apparently took her position very seriously.

"Oh please, be mild in your complaint to our master!" she pleaded with Alma.

The latter put her hand on the woman's arm. "I'm not going to complain," she said in a friendly tone. "There is really nothing to gripe about in this house. Everything just shines and glows with cleanliness. That the spider found its way into my room was surely just ... an accident."

The way Alma pronounced this statement, she probably believed it herself. I refrained from expressing any suspicion to the contrary.

While the household was coming to life and there was bustle everywhere, I went in search of Faustinius.

I found him in the horse stables of all places. Apparently he wanted to make sure that his favorite mount, a handsome white horse, had survived the sea voyage safe and sound.

The horse looked—to my untrained eye—chipper; Faustinius, on the other hand, seemed sleepy.

"I wanted to talk to you for a moment, old friend," I began. "It's about your barber...."

Faustinius patted the white horse's neck, but looked at me questioningly. "Lurco? What about him?"

The next moment he smiled as if he'd grasped something.

"Are you finally going to take me up on my offer and get a haircut after the latest fashion?" he said. "It would certainly help your chances with the ladies...."

"With the ladies?" I asked, against my will. Actually, I had wanted to talk to Faustinius about the incident last night. About Lurco, who had sneaked through corridors where he had no business to be, armed with a knife.

Faustinius slapped me in a comradely fashion with his hand on my shoulder.

"You are a clever fellow, Thanar. A man of honor. An able merchant. And the best friend a man could wish for. But when it comes to love—forgive me for putting it so bluntly—you are a bit...."

He fell silent and smiled at me patronizingly.

"Go ahead and say it," I grumbled. "You don't have to go easy on me."

Faustinius nodded. He squeezed my shoulder tighter.

"Layla," he began, then mercilessly continued, "she loves someone else, doesn't she?"

I winced. "How do you know?"

"Oh, please, old friend. I see how she often writes letters for hours ... looking very dreamy. And I see, too, that though you are dear to her, she does not burn with passion for you."

I nodded somberly. "I guess that's the way it is. But to return to Lurco...."

Faustinius ignored my objection.

"Your competitor—do you know him?" he asked. "What kind of man is he? Can he even hold a candle to you?"

I sighed.

Then I told him about Marcellus and my friendly relationship with him. And the intricate love triangle that connected me with him and Layla.

I found that being able to talk to a friend about this vexed matter made me feel better.

"Hmm," Faustinius said when I had finished. "So this Marcellus is young, aristocratic, handsome, and wealthy? What woman could resist such a man? But does he also possess your kind of spirit and wit, my friend?"

I nodded hesitantly. If one really wanted to grant me such qualities, then Marcellus certainly possessed them to the same extent.

On the contrary: especially when it came to Layla, I sometimes felt like a real dope. Spirit and wit my ass ... I was an old, lovesick fool, but nevertheless ready to finally shake off this pathetic condition.

A thoughtful expression settled over Faustinius's features.

"If you want my advice, old friend," he began, "we are often so spellbound by what we supposedly crave that we hold in far too low esteem the good and beautiful things we would merely have to reach for."

"Meaning?" I grumbled, although I thought I already knew what he was getting at.

I was to be proved right.

"Alma," he announced, smiling broadly. "She is no less beautiful and clever a woman than your Layla. And she is your kind: a barbarian from the north."

He grinned mischievously. "No, kidding aside, she's fond of you, I'm sure of it. If Lurco embellishes you a little more, brings out your strengths, you know...."

"But I don't want a new haircut," I replied, probably a little ill-tempered by now.

If it should finally be granted that I might conquer the heart of a woman, then I truly did not want her to take me because of my fashionable hairstyle.

"To get back to Lurco," I tried one more time to change the subject. "What I wanted to discuss with you...."

Now, at last, I was able to tell Faustinius my real concern. I repeated to him as verbatim as possible the report that Optimus had given me the previous night.

When I had finished, Faustinius laughed. So loudly and heartily that the white horse, whose neck he was still patting, reared up in fright.

"Lurco, a treacherous knife murderer?" Faustinius exclaimed. "No, my dear friend, you're barking up the wrong tree."

I found his outburst of mirth quite inappropriate.

"But Lurco couldn't—or wouldn't—tell us what he was

up to with the knife," I protested. "Or what he was doing in that part of the house at such a late hour. Yes, he denied being there at all. And this despite the fact that my Optimus even approached him!"

Faustinius raised his hands placatingly.

"That may be so, my friend. I certainly don't doubt your words. Or the reliability of your brave veteran. Lurco sometimes does behave ... well, a little strangely. One might think that the gods envy his flawless beauty and often haunt him with restless nights and many a dark dream. They drive him out of bed, make him wander, often without him even knowing about it later."

Faustinius actually seemed to be very familiar with his young slave, thus confirming my suspicion that Lurco was much more than a mere barber for him.

"You're saying he walks in his sleep?" I asked. "And that he carries a knife while doing so? Don't you find that a little, um, worrisome?"

It was said that people who wandered around at night without knowing about it later were controlled by dark forces, that they were possessed by a demon who guided their steps.

But Faustinius didn't seem to care. He shrugged.

"My Lurco would never ever hurt anyone," he said, a tender smile playing around the corners of his mouth. "I'd stake my life on that. He's such a squeamish fellow. And he can't stand the sight of blood, did you know that? Even when he gives me the tiniest cut while shaving—which truly doesn't happen often—he turns away in disgust. No, Thanar, whatever your Optimus may have observed, it was certainly of a harmless nature. I assure you of that."

What should I say in response to this passionate defense?

I took my leave of Faustinius and left him to his steed. But this didn't mean that he had convinced me of Lurco's innocence.

XII

The days in Alexandria flew by. We drifted through the busy streets of the metropolis, where people of every origin and skin color crowded together. Egyptians, Greeks, Romans, Jews—even merchants from faraway India lived and worked in the city.

We strolled along the canals, watched boats and ships being loaded and unloaded, and marveled at the range of goods on offer in the numerous markets. There were exotic spices, pepper, ginger, cinnamon from faraway India, garments made of fine cotton, the finest silks from China, papyrus produced in Egypt, and beguiling perfumes that made both Alma and Layla swoon. The merchant who hawked the fragrances made a small fortune from us.

The selection was altogether so varied that one quickly lost track, and so tempting that we returned home every evening with a lighter purse.

Alexandria had become—almost more than Rome itself—the center of international trade. Caravan routes converged there, and the most imposing cargo ships from all over the world lay at anchor on the city's miles-long quays. Carts, goods carriers and exotic pack animals crowded the streets, sending Alma into squeals of delight. She had a weakness for any kind of creature—well, except hairy spiders, of course! She was particularly fond of the camels with their bulging lips, strange humps and swaying gait.

Besides shopping, we naturally devoted ourselves to the real purpose of our trip: we marveled at the sights of the metropolis, which were just as diverse as the market offerings.

But my joy was not undimmed: during the first days in Alexandria, I found myself constantly thinking of Layla's words—her warning. I couldn't help but look out for dark omens with every step I took. And as is the case with signs of any kind, if you consciously searched for them, then of course you discovered them in great numbers.

In addition, I looked around every corner, into every open house entrance, every dark alley, to see if there might not be a danger lurking there for Alma. In every man who came too close to us, I thought I recognized an assassin. With every carriage that sped past us, I rushed to Alma's side to protect her.

I scolded myself for being a fool, forcing myself to turn my attention to our sightseeing, but a real lightheartedness would not set in anytime soon.

I couldn't forget the hairy spider that had given Alma such a fright, and I also caught Layla occasionally frowning and seeming to be thinking hard about something: something quite unpleasant.

Alma herself also confessed to me—it was on the third day of our visit—that night after night she was haunted by hideous dreams.

"I see it before me, the hairy carcass you impaled with your knife, Thanar," she whispered to me when we were alone for an hour. "And in my dreams it grows and grows until it fills my whole chamber! I am already tormented by the fear of even going to bed at night."

Several times the question had been on the tip of my tongue, of whether Alma had enemies, whether she perhaps knew of someone who might have played the evil trick with the tarantula on her. Or who might even want to take her life, and had suspected a deadly weapon in the exotic arachnid.

But just as I finally took heart and was about to speak on this heinous subject, Capito appeared next to us.

Alma and I were sitting on the rickety wooden benches in front of a snack bar, fortifying ourselves with spicy lamb skewers, when he suddenly took a seat at our side without being asked.

I had not seen him coming. Had he followed us? Had he waylaid us?

You can see how tense, how overheated my imagination was by now, that I was asking myself such questions.

In any case, Capito must have overheard Alma's last words, because he immediately came—and with a broad smile, this libertine!—to speak about the spider in question.

"It's a shame I couldn't see it with my own eyes," he lamented. "Was it really as big and hideous as everyone says? I would have loved to sketch it and use it for my new book. My *Guide to the Wonders of the World*! Of course, an overview of the hideous wildlife you encounter along the way can't be omitted. My readers—especially the female ones—love stories about monsters. And about brave barbarians who rescue noble ladies from these beasts!"

He eyed me with a mischievous glint in his eye.

Then he raised his head, stared at the sky, and announced in a theatrical voice: "*A truly terrible demon from the land of the necromancers*—that would be a fantastic caption, wouldn't it, my dear friends? I must find such a tarantula. A living specimen! No matter what the cost."

Alma shuddered, but Capito was not deterred.

He ran to the counter of the booth to grab some food and drink, and immediately returned with a cup of date wine and a massive slice of pyramid cake. This dessert seemed to be the most popular treat in Alexandria— although I couldn't help suspecting that it was sold exclusively to tourists.

Capito stuffed himself with a few bites of the rock-hard, sesame-sprinkled delicacy, then continued with a grin, "Who knows, maybe the spider was the pet of Petronius, our unknown host? Who would be surprised, in a country where people worship cats and dogs as gods? Petronius may soon send hired assassins after us when we sail up the Nile and he returns home to his villa. He will be beside himself when he learns what you have done to his darling, oh brave Germanic!"

Against my will, I had to laugh. It was good to make fun of the incident with the monster spider instead of suspecting a sinister murder plot behind it. At least, I had to admit that much.

"I've met people on my travels who kept the craziest pets," the chatterbox continued good-humoredly, "monkeys, roosters, quails, crows, parrots, cheetahs, foxes ... even toads and snakes. Why not a spider, too?"

"No one in their right mind would willingly let such a

hairy monster into their home," Alma protested.

Capito waved it off.

"Oh, my dear lady, people love the hideous. And the monstrous! And isn't everything in Egypt much too big? And sometimes quite abominable? Wait until you see the Nile crocodiles! Deadly beasts with jaws full of sharp teeth and a scale-armored tail with which they can beat a full-grown man to death. They grow up to thirty feet long, can you imagine?"

He spread his arms, probably to emphasize the indescribable dimensions. "These beasts can consume a human in one piece and still not be full afterwards!"

As much as Capito's endless ramblings strained my mind, I have to confess that he was cheering us up with his madcap stories.

My tension eased, and I saw Alma smile more often over the next few days. It seemed as if we could finally leave behind the dark omens that had seemed to haunt us.

Had the generous sacrifices I'd made at just about every temple, and all the donations I'd given to the priests, finally swayed the gods in our favor?

There were no new incidents in the next few days behind which one might have suspected the work of an assassin. No further vermin found their way into Petronius's villa.

Alma slept better again, while I began to convince myself that perhaps the spider had gotten into Alma's bed by itself after all.

And that the brick that had almost killed the beautiful widow in Rhodos had only been due to a dilapidated roof.

Even the spoiled date dish might not have been anything worse in the end than an oversight on the part of the cooks. In the southern heat, food spoiled easily, possibly even the otherwise durable sweet dates. And reckless drivers, like the one who'd almost run Alma over ... well, they could be found in almost every town. Even this villain—soberly seen—need not have been a hired scoundrel who had sought her life.

In any case, we devoted ourselves, ever more carefree and with growing enthusiasm, to the wonders of Alexandria. The women were drawn to the magnificent tombs of Alexander the Great and the legendary Cleopatra, the last pharaoh to rule Egypt. Layla believed that Cleopatra had not in fact been a dark sorceress, as was generally said.

"I think she was just a passionate woman who loved two great men," Layla explained to me. "The Romans do her an injustice by condemning her like that!" With these words, she gave me a look I couldn't interpret.

Next we visited the sanctuary of Pan, the eternally lustful lord of the forests, perched on a man-made hill. A winding road led us up and offered us a royal, panoramic view of the entire metropolis.

As I stood up there, with Alma, Layla, and friend Faustinius at my side, and for once neither Capito nor Timotheos in sight ... ah, I thought myself invincible, close to the immortals, indeed blessed by their favor.

Not even the view of the massive necropolises that surrounded Alexandria, where everything revolved around death and embalming and the strange burial rites of the Egyptians, could dampen my spirits. Not a single dark cloud on the horizon announced the disaster that was soon to befall us.

On another day we directed our steps to the south, in the direction of Lake Mareotis, and visited the largest and most imposing temple of Alexandria. It was called the *Sarapeion* and was dedicated to the god Sarapis.

To the Greeks he was Zeus, to the Romans Jupiter, and a hundred steps had to be climbed to reach his sanctuary. Crowds of people in search of healing and oracles thronged the courtyards and squares, and moved between the pools of water in the temple complex.

The interior of the temple itself was decorated with slabs of gold, silver and bronze.

But the undisputed highlight of the city was the *Museion*—on this Alma, Layla and I agreed.

The Museion was a place of learning for scholars, poets and researchers from all over the world. The great Archimedes and the equally famous Euclid had once worked in these venerable halls, which were dedicated to the Muses. And even today, one could study at the Museion among the most famous sages. Literature, mathematics, astronomy, and medicine were the disciplines taught and studied here with holy zeal.

The heart of the Museion, however, was the world-famous Library of Alexandria. More than half a million scrolls were available here, and a guide who gave us the information even claimed that the endless storerooms of the great library contained a copy of every work ever put on papyrus by any poet or scholar. This sounded a bit like our good Capito telling another of his anecdotes, but none of us contradicted the venerable sage.

In the reading halls, hundreds of students murmured incessantly to themselves as they read. It was like walking through the middle of an angry swarm of bees.

Gardens full of plants and animals from all over the world adjoined the complex, and at night you could look up at the stars from the observatory.

I think Layla would have loved to move into the Museion, never to leave it again.

XIII

We had planned to spend ten days in Alexandria, then to head further south. The time passed much too quickly. And I had to realize to my displeasure that Timotheos, Faustinius's scribbler, was occupying Alma more and more.

Even during the first few days in town, he was constantly pawing around her, whenever I turned away for a moment. I probably shouldn't have been surprised. After all, he had been wooing her since Halicarnassus. But he became more and more bold—and pushy—in his courtship.

He offered to show her this or that sight, bought her small—very small!—gifts in the markets and stores, and engaged her in endless conversations about the wonders of the city. Alma seemed to enjoy his attention very much. It seemed to me that she met him with the same kindness she displayed towards myself.

Layla, of course, didn't miss my jealous glances at the scribe, which also should not have surprised me. As I have already described, absolutely nothing ever escaped her attention. At least, that's how it appeared to me.

She didn't miss the opportunity to comment on Timotheos's courtship of Alma once she and I were alone and undisturbed for an hour. Layla was not a woman who kept her opinions to herself, even though she always knew how to express herself gently and spare my feelings.

This time, however, her comments were surprisingly positive.

"Alma seems really fond of you," she said.

At first I thought I had misheard her. I had expected that she wanted to comfort me, that she would tell me how Alma was much more interested in Timotheos than in me, and that I shouldn't get my hopes up. That much was obvious, wasn't it?

Having reproached Layla just a few days ago for so obviously trying to set me up with Alma—well, I had conveniently forgotten it by then. Or simply ignored it. After all, a man was allowed to change his mind, wasn't he?

Still, I couldn't figure out what Layla was trying to tell me.

"Alma is fond of me?" I repeated incredulously. "Then why does she seek the company of this scribe?"

"It is he who seeks her company, Thanar," Layla replied. "Not the other way around."

"Granted. But Alma could shake him off if she wanted to, couldn't she? If his favors were annoying to her?"

Layla winked at me. "Don't you notice how she keeps gazing over at you, and is always seeking our company? Even when Timotheos doesn't leave her side?"

"Yes ... I do. But she's your friend, Layla. I thought it was your company she was looking for."

Layla gave me a pitying smile—and I turned away. Once again, I felt like a fool.

This had to stop!

As our stay progressed, however, the friendship between Alma and the scribbler seemed to deepen.

There was also nothing wrong with Timotheos personally—except that I found him unsympathetic and overly pompous, as I said. He was quite a handsome and educated fellow. And Alma had every right to a new union after her first marriage, which had probably not been particularly happy. Nevertheless, Timotheos did not seem to me to be the right man for her.

Not your business, I silently rebuked myself. After all, I was not Alma's father or brother, who would have had a say in her love affairs.

Layla, on the other hand, was more and more occupied by Capito. He obviously had no amorous intentions with her—he just seemed to be looking for someone who would lend a sympathetic ear to his hair-raising stories. He talked and talked and talked.

He seemed to have the right adventurous anecdote ready for every topic, every occasion. And, of course, the right joke.

Elithios Phoitetes chats with two friends. One says, "I think it's wrong to slaughter sheep, because they provide us with wool for our clothes and blankets."

The second adds, "We shouldn't kill cows either, because they provide us with milk and cheese."

Elithios finally agrees with the two: "And we shouldn't slaughter pigs either, because they provide us with so much delicious meat."

Layla actually seemed to be amused by such antics. She laughed a lot. At least she wasn't continually indulging in dark and murderous thoughts, I told myself—and went out of the way of the two of them. I enjoyed Layla's company, but was not prepared to let Capito talk my ears off in return.

It did not escape my attention that since that night with the spider, my faithful Optimus had been keeping an unobtrusive, yet persistent, eye on Faustinius's barber.

Lurco spent most of his time strolling around near his master, even though I had the impression that he did not like our sightseeing very much. He protected his immaculately pale skin with the help of a parasol and seemed very uncomfortable in the crowds of the markets and streets. But wherever I saw him, Optimus was usually not far away either.

My faithful veteran of the legion never seemed to sleep. During the day, he spied on Lurco in the manner I described, when he wasn't escorting Layla or myself. And at night, too, I met him in the hallway at almost every hour when I happened to leave my room.

On these occasions, I always sent him to bed with stern words. Again and again I reminded him that although he was in charge of my guard, he did not have to take over every shift himself. Apart from that, the palace of Petronius was secured by strong walls and gates, as well as its own guard. We were not threatened by any danger.

"No danger from *outside,* sir," Optimus once commented on my statement to that effect.

I pretended not to hear the remark. I would not let myself be carried away again by gloomy forebodings and unpleasant speculations!

As the days went by, however, my words seemed to bear fruit, and Optimus allowed himself a somewhat less rigorous performance of his duties.

Soon I saw him talking or playing dice with other servants or slaves, and eventually he even seemed to strike up a delicate bond of friendship with Lurco.

On one of the last evenings in Alexandria, when I visited the servants' quarters to discuss something with one of my coachmen, I actually discovered Optimus under the knives of Lurco. That is, he was having his hair cut by the young barber!

With Timotheos, on the other hand, I had a less pleasant encounter. The second afternoon we spent in the Museion library, I found myself alone for a moment in the company of the scribe.

I don't know what got into me, but I made the spontaneous—and rather ill-considered—decision to use this opportunity for sounding him out a bit about his intentions with Alma. As if that wasn't obvious enough?

I stepped up next to him and looked over his shoulder at the scroll he was studying. What exactly he was reading there, I did not take in at all. It was some treatise in Greek—which I knew, but didn't particularly like.

"Alma's a very attractive woman, isn't she?" I got straight to the point.

Timotheos raised his head, lowered the scroll with paralyzing slowness, looked at me and nodded.

"And very well-read she is, too," I continued. "She loves this place as much as any learned man."

I pointed with a sweeping gesture to the endless shelves that surrounded us. Every single one of them was literally crammed with scrolls.

Timotheos frowned.

"Erudition should be reserved for us men," he said. "After all, only we possess the necessary intellect for it. And as for beauty, if I have my way, the pearls on a woman's ears are dearer to me than the most beautiful face."

He grinned condescendingly at me.

In general, he was quite an arrogant fellow. He was a freedman and now in Faustinius' paid service, but that did not give him the right to use such a tone towards me! As if I were some immature youngster he could look down upon. Undoubtedly he saw me as a competitor, but he obviously considered himself superior to me by far.

"Pearls?" I repeated incredulously.

He put on a pitying expression—as if he had suddenly realized that I was slow on the uptake on top of everything else.

"Money, my friend," he sneered. "A well-filled purse. That's a woman's finest adornment, don't you think? A widow's fortune ... promising her new husband a comfortable life."

He laughed. Then he turned back to his reading.

Disgruntled, I left the room.

XIV

Finally turning our backs on Alexandria, we embarked on a luxurious and spacious Nile barque, which Faustinius had hired all to ourselves, and followed the Canopus Canal in a southeasterly direction.

Along this stretch of water, taverns, dance halls and places of revelry were set like gems on a necklace. It was a mile of vice like no other, but we did not linger.

Finally we reached Heliopolis, where once the legendary Plato was supposed to have studied for more than a decade of his life.

The pharaohs had built a mighty temple here in honor of Re, their sun god, but only its ruins remained. The once great city was little more than a place for ghosts.

Faustinius instructed his army of slaves to set up camp for the night a little way outside the city, near the banks of the Nile. As always, the men complied with his order quickly and very efficiently. Within an hour, everything was ready for us, and meat was already sizzling over the fire, smelling delicious.

As happened every evening, Faustinius's cooks treated us to the finest delicacies. They had stocked up on local fish and meat, fresh vegetables and Oriental spices at the markets of Alexandria.

We dined like the gods on Mount Olympus and soon retired to our tents sluggish and satiated—no, overstuffed!

I fell asleep as soon as I had made myself comfortable on

my couch. The days, filled with so many new impressions, had probably tired me more than a little.

Long before Apollo let his sun chariot rise above the horizon the next morning, my night's rest was to come to an abrupt end.

I heard voices when I was at first still half asleep, which made me think of dream-images. But then suddenly someone barked some strange orders in a loud and commanding voice.

"Bring water and clean cloths! Quickly! Come on, what are you waiting for? Who had the last watch? You two, right? You'll have to answer for yourselves! You there, lad, don't stand there gawping! Better wake your master!" And so on.

I quickly slipped on a tunic and staggered out of my tent.

I looked around in the darkness of the camp, which was lit only by a few oil lanterns. Slaves were running around in wild confusion. Women's voices wailed, men whispered to each other, seemingly shocked.

The man yelling the orders was Optimus.

He was kneeling at the edge of our camp, not far from my tent, and was bent over a motionless figure.

When he saw me, he jumped up and came rushing toward me.

"I'm glad you're awake, sir!" he cried breathlessly. "I was just about to send for you. There ... has been an attack."

Without waiting for my answer, he turned and ran back to the place where he had been kneeling just moments before.

I followed him quickly.

As I stepped closer, I recognized the figure lying motionless on the ground. It was Timotheos the scribbler. My competitor.

Optimus bent over him, searching for his pulse and listening for his breathing. "I found him here, half dead, a few moments ago," he explained to me with a quick glance over his shoulder.

More guards came rushing over.

Optimus grabbed the stack of cloths one of the men had brought with him. He wrapped two of them into a thick compress. Then he waved one of the other men over, and with his help turned the limp body of the scribe to the side. He then pressed the compress onto a gaping wound in Timotheos' back.

The scribe gasped. Then he spat blood. It was a foul-smelling, dark red slime that poured out of his mouth and immediately seeped into the sandy ground.

He was still alive, but I realized that he was doomed to die. There could be no doubt about that.

The back of his robe was drenched, and when I looked more closely, I discovered two more puncture wounds from which the scribe's life was escaping remorselessly. The incisions were narrow and perhaps not deep, but blood was continually seeping from all his wounds, staining the sand at our feet red.

Optimus folded up more compresses and struggled to doctor the scribe as best he could. But when he gave me a sideways glance, I knew he was thinking the same thing I was.

Timotheos was beyond saving. He was already as pale as

a dead man. He had lost too much blood for any mortal to save him, not even the best physician—even if one had been on hand.

Optimus nodded his head toward the center of the wounded man's body. "Look, Thanar! The money pouch he always wore on his belt is missing. Probably he was attacked by desert robbers."

"Who inflicted such wounds on him? Just for a few coins?" I asked doubtfully.

"To these dogs, a human life doesn't count for much," Optimus replied with a growl.

Behind us, the entire camp seemed to have come to life in the meantime. Faustinius came rushing up, swarmed by some servants. Close behind him followed Layla, Alma, Zenobia and Capito.

I knelt down next to Timotheos and took his hand.

He fixed his eyes, which seemed dull and almost lifeless, on me in a final effort.

"What befell you, man?" I asked him. "Tell us what happened!"

He gasped. Once again blood gathered in the corners of his mouth.

He opened his lips, tried to speak, but his strength left him. A last breath escaped his throat before the life finally stole out of his body. His lips formed a single, barely audible word.

"Alma."

His hand suddenly felt limp in mine, his eyes went rigid and looked dead into space.

Alma let out a strangled cry. She put her hands in front of her face, while Zenobia grabbed her around the waist for support.

In the next moment, however, Alma had broken away from her slave, turned and run away sobbing.

Zenobia looked at me, startled, but then she hurried after her mistress.

XV

For a few moments we all stood paralyzed, then Faustinius took the initiative. With a few terse words, inadequately hiding his emotions, he gave instructions to take Timotheos's body away.

"He was ... a friend," he spoke to me haltingly after his servants had hurried off with their sad burden. "I will see that he is given a proper burial. Here in a foreign land, alas, but as far as I know he had no loved ones left back home either."

He didn't say a word about it, didn't ask any questions about how and why Timotheos might have died. But I could see that it was working behind his forehead. Just as it was behind mine.

What had Timotheos wanted to tell us with his last words? Had I even understood him correctly? Had he really died with Alma's name on his lips?

"Let's talk later, my friend," Faustinius said to me. He put his hand on my shoulder, as he was so fond of doing, then walked away.

The others who had rushed over also returned to their tents or to their work, even if Optimus had to nudge some guards and servants a bit. With agitated arm movements and brusque commands, he shooed them away, and finally they shuffled off. But their lamenting and chatter would not cease. There was talk of a curse with which the dark Egyptian gods were pursuing us. Of sorcerers, demons, and necromancers, who had demanded a sacrifice from within our midst.

In the end, Layla and I were the only ones left standing at the edge of the camp where Timotheos had died, and only the bloodstained earth still reminded us of his sad fate.

Layla held a lamp in her hands, while I had a slave bring me a torch. Together, our lights illuminated the darkness enough for us to make out a trail in the sand. It could be followed a short distance into the desert beyond our camp, but then it was lost in the dunes.

"So Timotheos did indeed return from the desert," I said to Layla. "He must have been attacked there—and then dragged himself back all the way here with his last ounces of strength. But what, by all the gods, was he doing out there in the middle of the night?"

Someone cleared his throat behind me.

I turned around and recognized Optimus. I had not been aware that the veteran had stayed by our side.

With a quick wave of my hand, I tried to dismiss him. "See that you get some more sleep, my good fellow," I said to him. "There's nothing more you can do here, I'm afraid."

Optimus stepped from one foot to the other. "There is something I would like to discuss with you, sir," he said. "I'm afraid it won't tolerate any delay."

His tone made me prick up my ears and take notice.

"Oh? What's the matter?" I asked. "What's on your mind?"

He gave Layla a telling look, which could only mean one thing: he would have preferred to tell me what he had to say in private.

"If it has to do with this," I said as I pointed my hand to the discolored ground, "you shouldn't be afraid to speak in front of Layla. She is a woman with a keen sense for crime."

What unfortunate phrasing, went through my head, but the words had already been spoken. And they were true, as much as that might astonish a conservative man like Optimus. Or rather: as much as it still astonished me.

The veteran frowned, but he did as he was told. A man like him would never have questioned the words of a superior. Still, Optimus seemed to have reservations about speaking freely in front of Layla. His gaze flitted over her features, but then he fixed it on me.

"Timotheos's last words," he began, "I think I know what they mean."

"That his last thoughts were of Alma?" interjected Layla.

"That much is obvious," I said. "The only question is: why?"

Timotheos had not died with Alma's name on his lips because of his love and care for her. That much I knew. He had made no secret—at least to me—that he saw nothing more than a financially favorable match in the beautiful widow.

"I think I can answer that very question," Optimus took the floor again. "Because it was probably for Alma that he went out into the desert at such a late hour."

"You can't be serious!" I exclaimed.

But Optimus nodded emphatically.

"It so happened," he began, "that in the early hours of the night I took the watch on this side of the camp."

This was nothing unusual so far. When we slept under

the open sky, our guards divided the various posts around the camp and the guard shifts among themselves, regardless of whether the respective man was in Faustinius's service or belonged to one of the other travelers.

Optimus and my other guards participated in this routine. This meant that they had shorter duty periods overall, without our safety suffering as a result.

At least that was the theory. In practice, the death of the scribe had just taught us otherwise. Our sense of security had proven to be deceptive.

Optimus continued, "I saw Timotheos sneaking out of his tent at a late hour and getting ready to head out into the desert. I was, well, puzzled as to where he was going in the middle of the night, so I ran after him and asked him if everything was all right. Of course, it is not my business what the servants of Faustinius are up to. How and where—or even with whom—they spend the hours of the night. But as I said, his behavior seemed strange to me."

"And what was his reply?" I asked.

What man in his right mind would voluntarily seek the way into the desert at night? It must have been clear to Timotheos that he was risking his neck, even if he perhaps lacked the experience with exotic journeys in general and the Egyptian desert in particular.

For a brief moment, Optimus' gaze flitted over Layla's face.

When he spoke again, he directed his words exclusively to me: "Timotheos was ... how shall I say it?"

He interrupted himself briefly, seeming to search for the

appropriate words. Then he continued: "Well, he seemed to be in a good mood. He had a date with a pretty little bird, he told me. One with whom he was going to build a nest very soon."

"Those were his exact words?"

"Yes, sir," Optimus replied, averting his eyes from me and looking down at the ground in dismay.

I had trouble hiding my astonishment—or should I say my horror?

"I assumed he was talking about Alma," Optimus added in his most discreet tone. His eyes remained fixed on the tips of his shoes. I could tell he was as uncomfortable with this conversation as I was.

Even Layla reacted with astonishment: "A tryst in the desert, you say? And in the middle of the night? You believed that? Surely Alma would never have agreed to such an appointment."

Optimus said nothing in reply.

I eyed Layla, trying to read the intention behind her words. Was she just saying that because she wanted to spare my feelings? Did she want to make me believe that Alma was only interested in me and that she was only using Timotheos's attention to arouse my jealousy?

On the other hand, I would have judged Alma in the same way. Arranging a nocturnal tryst in the desert just wasn't like her. She loved adventure, new experiences, the extraordinary. That much was true. But she was also reserved, sometimes even a little afraid. Simply because, I suspected, she had led a very sheltered existence up until this point.

I shook my head. Did anyone understand women? In the

end, perhaps I should take Faustinius as a model and give my favor to a hairless youth who would consent to sweeten my lonely nights. That was at least uncomplicated.

Optimus cleared his throat.

"If I understood Timotheos correctly," he said, "Alma did not merely agree to the meeting. On the contrary, he indicated that the secret tryst had been *her* idea. She sent him a letter inviting him, and he himself seemed quite surprised about such a request, if I may say so. At least that was my impression."

"Impossible!" I protested before I could stop myself. This was getting more and more insane. I could not and would not believe it!

Suddenly I felt reminded of that terrible time not so long ago, the days when I had given Layla her freedom—in the hope that from then on she would live with me voluntarily and out of love. How bitterly I'd been disappointed then ... and now again? This time by another woman, whose affection was supposedly mine alone, as Layla was claiming so stubbornly?

Optimus was silent for a moment and stepped uneasily from one leg to the other.

Then he continued—in a deadpan tone—"I thought that maybe Alma had suggested this night meeting away from the camp because she wanted to meet Timotheos secretly."

Now, at last, he raised his head and looked me in the eyes again. "It seemed to me sir, if I may say so, that Alma has turned her favor toward the scribe in the last few days. Whereas before, well, she seemed rather devoted to you. I really don't want to pass judgment on that, though!"

"Yes, yes, all right," I replied. It was touching how the good Optimus was trying to spare me.

"That may be why Alma wanted to meet her new suitor away from the camp," he added. "So you wouldn't know, Thanar. Women are fickle creatures," he added bitterly.

Optimus was unmarried, but apparently he hadn't had too many good experiences with the female sex. But could he be right about Alma and Timotheos? Had they gotten together secretly because the beautiful widow didn't want to hurt my feelings?

"Did you see Alma leave her tent?" I asked Optimus. "To meet Timotheos?"

He shook his head.

"No, sir. I am sorry. My watch ended shortly after I spoke to Timotheos, and I must confess that I went to sleep. Here near your tent, Thanar."

He pointed with his hand to a spot just a few steps away from us. One or two crumpled blankets lay there on the ground. Next to them stood an oil lamp.

Optimus continued, "I woke up again only when I heard moaning sounds that seemed very close. That was Timotheos dragging himself back here half dead. He must have been wandering around the desert bleeding. Perhaps he also lost consciousness for a short while after being attacked."

He interrupted himself and seemed to be thinking about something.

"That would fit," he said then, "the sequence of events, I mean. His wounds were not so severe that he would have succumbed to them on the spot. If he had found his way back to camp more quickly, we might have been able to save him."

I nodded wordlessly. Optimus was undoubtedly right; a veteran of the legions knew better than any of us about wounds of all kinds.

"I'll ask the men who were on duty after me if they noticed anything," he added. "Maybe one of them saw Alma when she left the camp."

He sounded as if he were tormented by a guilty conscience for not being able to give me a more satisfactory answer.

"Don't bother," I said. "I'm going to talk to Alma directly. Right now."

Alma had suffered a shock when she had witnessed Timotheos breathe his last. That had been all too clear. To tear her from sleep now—if she was sleeping at all—was cruel.

If I had been in a milder mood, I would not have bothered her for the next few hours, but I was dying to have answers.

I wanted to hear from her own mouth that she had not come up with such an insane plan as Timotheos had claimed. The scribe must have lied to Optimus; that was the only reasonable explanation that entered my head.

But then why had Timotheos died with Alma's name on his lips?

XVI

I immediately put my plan into action. I strode to Alma's tent, determined not to wait for daybreak. I wouldn't find sleep again anyway—and I didn't grant her any either at that moment.

One of Alma's men was keeping watch in front of the tent, but he didn't stop me.

As I carefully tugged at the tarp covering the entrance, I ran into Zenobia. Or rather, I almost tripped over her. She had probably been sleeping at the threshold of the tent entrance. Always near her mistress, like a faithful watchdog.

She got up, smoothed out her robe and looked at me in alarm. As was to be expected, she objected to my untimely visit. She spoke politely, not forgetting her position, but at the same time resolutely blocking my way.

But then Alma herself appeared, emerging from the darkness of the tent like a vision. Her long blond hair fell untamed over her shoulders, and dark circles showed around her beautiful eyes.

Gently but firmly, she pushed Zenobia aside. Yes, she even sent her out of the tent, leaving the two of us all alone.

I didn't even entertain the hope of finding the appropriate words for my request, so I just blurted out, "Did you make a date with Timotheos tonight?"

Alma's eyes widened. I was not able to tell whether it was

fear or anger that was reflected in them—or something else entirely?

It took quite a while before her lips opened. Slowly she began to speak, "I ... was not aware that I owed you an account, Thanar."

Her voice was gentle, but the look she gave me pained me. I read in it that she was all too familiar with male condescension, and that she detested being treated in this way.

Nevertheless, I was not going to back out now.

"Timotheos was murdered, Alma," I said as gently as I could. "That's why it's important to know what lured him out into the desert. Where he met his terrible end."

Her features hardened. "And you think it was me who ... *lured* him? You're not serious, I hope?"

"Timotheos mentioned that you had written him a letter, inviting him to a secret tryst away from the camp. That was the reason he left his tent this night—and ran to his death."

Alma shook her head. "Whoever claims such a thing is lying," she said.

She had now narrowed her eyes and was looking at me suspiciously. *Like an animal that feels cornered,* went through my head.

"Timotheos himself claimed that," I replied. "He was seen—and approached—when he left the camp."

"Well, then that person is lying, whoever it may have been who supposedly spoke to Timotheos."

She took a step toward me. A little of the old gentleness returned to her features.

"You should know, Thanar," she began, "that my heart

was not attached to Timotheos. I liked him, it is true. He was a kind and educated man. I enjoyed his company—by *day*, within proper limits. But not beyond that."

She gave me a meaningful look that I was not quite able to interpret.

I felt ashamed, like a jealous husband, which was not my nature at all.

I left Alma with a muttered farewell, and sucked in the cool morning air as I stood under the open sky again. The horizon was gradually starting to turn to gray.

One thing was certain: *someone* had indeed lied. The only question was, who? Alma—Timotheos—or even my faithful Optimus?

Of these three, it could only have been Timotheos. He must have invented Alma's letter—just to have an excuse to hand when Optimus approached him.

Probably he'd conceived the letter out of the need to justify himself, simply using the first idea that had come to mind. After all, it was no secret that *he* had been courting Alma.

Yes, that had to be the explanation. The only question was what the scribe had actually wanted in the desert tonight?

If you arranged to meet someone at a godforsaken place at a late hour, you hardly had anything respectable in mind. I knew that from my own experience. One or the other of my trade deals, which I had concluded in the past ... well, let's say when I was breaking a law or two, I'd always done it under the cover of darkness.

I stood around helplessly for a while, then it was my stomach, of all things, that snapped me out of my gloomy musings. It spoke up with a hungry rumble.

I decided to get some bread and cheese and immediately directed my steps towards the campfire hearth and the tent where our supplies were kept.

A young maid was already at work, probably preparing the morning meal. She was startled when I entered the tent, but when I told her what I wanted, she provided me with a generous portion of cheese and a small flatbread. I thanked her and returned outside.

I settled down on one of the comfortable rugs near the fireplace and started to devour my meal, but without real appetite.

Just as I was about to get up again, Faustinius appeared.

He joined me and had a sumptuous breakfast served by the slaves who had accompanied him.

"Good to meet you, Thanar," he began as he shoved nuts and olives into his mouth. "I couldn't go back to sleep, though I feel absolutely whacked. I guess we're not getting any younger, huh? And before we know it, it could all be over."

He shook his head and pointed out into the desert where his scribe had met such an abrupt end.

I really didn't feel like indulging in melancholy reflections on human mortality. I was tormented by completely different, far more earthly worries. Had Alma been Timotheos's lover? Was she a liar? Had the scribe become the victim of bandits—or was a cold-blooded murderer hiding in our midst, among those with whom I was friendly? That was probably my greatest concern.

"Did you want to discuss something with me, Faustinius?" I began. "I had the impression that something was on your mind ... earlier, when we found Timotheos."

He had withdrawn quickly after the death of the scribe. Too quickly. He had not asked a single question, although his head must have been as full of them as mine. But before he had gone, he had given me a strange look. I had not forgotten that.

Faustinius nodded. He looked around to see if we were unobserved. With a quick wave of his hand, he sent away the slave who was kneeling at his side—ready to read his master's every wish from his eyes.

When the fellow had departed, Faustinius looked at me with a serious expression.

"You know I put a lot of stock in your advice, Thanar," he said. "The death of my scribe is a terrible thing. To be stabbed in so cowardly a fashion, from behind, and under the cloak of darkness, without the slightest possibility of defending himself...."

He broke off and grimaced in disgust. In the process, he dropped the olive he had been about to eat back into its silver bowl.

"I do not wish to wrong anyone," he said after a short pause, "or even to accuse anybody of a crime they may not have committed. I ask you, therefore, also for your silence when you have heard me out. Not a word to anyone, will you?"

I nodded and signaled my agreement. His ominous words sent a cold shiver down my spine.

Faustinius looked around one more time, then said, "I had entrusted my Timotheos with a, well, somewhat delicate task. It was only a few days ago...."

He faltered and brought the olive back toward his mouth. He seemed to be thinking about how best to choose his next words.

XVII

My patience wasn't great that morning.

"Out with it!" I challenged him. "What was the task in question?"

Faustinius swallowed and dried his lips with a finely knitted mouth towel. A little oil still shone on them, giving my old friend the appearance of a man of luxury more than ever.

"Timotheos was tasked with spying on our chatty friend," he said then.

"Capito?" I asked incredulously.

Faustinius nodded with a thin smile.

"It is a most vexatious matter, I assure you. I truly consider myself a generous man, who gives freely whatever may be asked of him. So I definitely cannot stand to be robbed. And I ... well, I suspected, nay, I still suspect, Capito of stealing from me. More than that, I believe he is a professional thief! So now you know. Since he has been with us, my slaves have reported to me more than once about his misdeeds. Several of them saw him sneaking around in places where he had no business to be. In my tent, for example, near my money chest. And in similar places that an honest fellow would not dream of going."

He reached for the mouth cloth again. This time, however, he dabbed his forehead with it. Which seemed nonsensical to me. He could not possibly already be sweating. The cold of the night still lingered in my bones.

Faustinius continued, "None of my slaves, of course, dared to catch Capito in the act, red-handed, so to speak. They are all well-bred fellows who would never embarrass a guest of my house. Or in this case, a member of my traveling party. Especially not when they couldn't be absolutely sure what Capito actually intended. So they were behaving in a way that I approve of in principle."

He shrugged his shoulders. "Thus, I have no proof that their accusations are really true. However, I think highly of my slaves. They are not a scheming bunch with an overly fanciful imagination, if you know what I mean. I trust their word."

"And so you instructed your scribe to spy on Capito?" I concluded. "To find irrefutable proof of his guilt?"

"Right. Timotheos himself had already caught our chatterer snooping around in my chambers once. It was in Alexandria, only a few days ago. That's when I had enough, and I told Timotheos not to let Capito out of his sight again."

"So, was he successful?"

"That's just it," said Faustinius. "He died before he could tell me anything concrete or bring me any proof of my suspicions. But now, of course, I wonder—"

Again he interrupted himself. "As I said, I hate making accusations based merely on conjecture...."

My own scruples about this were limited. After all, we were talking in private, and a few purely theoretical considerations had to be allowed.

"You wonder," I completed my friend's words, "if Capito perhaps discovered your scribe's intentions—and has silenced him before Timotheos could unmask him?"

Faustinius nodded slowly. "That's not too far-fetched, is it? Perhaps Capito was caught red-handed by Timotheos ... and wanted to prevent his machinations from being exposed at all costs? I just don't understand what prompted my scribe to direct his steps into the desert—that's where he was ambushed, if I understand it correctly. Wasn't he? Could it be that he was following Capito? Was the scoundrel about to escape from the camp? But what chance did he think he would have—at night, alone, on foot?"

I pondered for a moment. Then I decided to take Faustinius into my confidence. I recounted to him the report that Optimus had given me—about Timotheos's alleged nocturnal rendezvous with Alma.

When I had finished, Faustinius frowned.

"I'm really sorry about that, old chap," he said hesitantly. "I thought the world of Timotheos. He was a fine fellow. But that Alma would choose him over you ... I honestly wouldn't have thought so. Who can understand women?" he added with a touch of passion.

His words sounded like an echo of my own thoughts.

He patted me comfortingly on the shoulder. "I guess you're really unlucky in love, poor friend. If I may say so."

His pity was the last thing I wanted.

"Looks like," I grumbled. "But that's not what I'm concerned with right now. Don't you see how it could have happened? Timotheos left his tent at night to meet Alma. And Capito could have followed him. A man leaving camp alone, unarmed, and under cover of darkness—what better opportunity could there have been for a villain determined to do his worst? If Timotheos had indeed gathered evidence against our chatterer, then the latter may have seen the perfect opportunity to silence him, no matter the cost."

I spoke quickly and emphatically. When I had finished, I was left breathless.

Faustinius nodded in understanding, but then scratched his temple.

"A terrible notion," he said. "But are we really allowed to imply that Capito would be capable of such an outrage? I mean, he's a show-off and all ... and maybe a common thief, too. But a *murderer*? Besides, Timotheos would have come to me after all, if he'd found any proof. Or even caught Capito red-handed. Don't you think?"

"Not necessarily," I said. "Timotheos may have been a trustworthy and capable scribe to you, but I also know that he was greedy for money. He had already succeeded in buying his freedom as your slave, but now that he was planning his future on his own two feet—he might have wanted to pad his coffers a little. Not merely through a possible marriage to a rich widow like Alma. What man wants to be dependent on a woman when he can acquire his own wealth?"

"You think my loyal scribe might have tried to blackmail Capito? Instead of reporting to me?" Faustinius asked incredulously.

He didn't fancy the idea one bit. You could see that clearly in his face.

I, however, liked it all the more, because I still didn't want to believe that Timotheos had actually been on a date with Alma. With Capito a new possibility suddenly opened up. One that I liked much better.

What if Timotheos had actually collected evidence of Capito's thieving machinations—and wanted to blackmail the chatterbox with it? Couldn't he then have arranged to meet *him* at night in the desert? To offer him, in exchange for a generous sum—or even a share of the loot—to turn a blind eye and let Capito off unscathed? By which, of course, he would have committed treason against his master, Faustinius. But that didn't seem to have stopped him.

The desert wasteland was the right place for such a shameful trade pact, and the midnight hour would have been the right time.

Timotheos could not admit this true reason for his nocturnal excursion to my Optimus, of course, if he did not want to make himself suspicious. For this reason, he had quickly invented the tryst with Alma—and thus deceived my guard.

Yes, that was a good fit. That's how it must have happened, I was almost sure.

Nevertheless, I kept this suspicion to myself for the time being. I didn't want to posthumously sully Timotheos's reputation as long as I had nothing more than conjecture to show.

Instead, I made a suggestion to Faustinius.

"If it is all right with you," I said, "I will assign my Optimus to continue spying on Capito. My able veteran is the man for the job. And he knows how to defend himself should he put himself in danger in the process."

Faustinius immediately agreed. Yes, he seemed downright relieved.

"But please see that Optimus is warned," he added. "That

he goes about his work with extreme caution! I would never forgive myself if anything happened to another of our men."

After taking my leave of Faustinius, I looked around for Layla.

To my horror, I spotted her a good two hundred paces from the camp between the dunes. She was apparently following Timotheos's trail, but at least one of my guards was at her side.

The sun had finally risen over the walls of Heliopolis, which were only a stone's throw from our camp. The green-blue waters of the Nile were glistening in the first light of the morning.

I ran after Layla, following her and the guard, realizing that her footprints in the sand actually went parallel to the trail that the mortally wounded Timotheos must have left on his way back to camp.

During the night we had lost the track, but now it was more clearly recognizable, although the wind had blown it over almost beyond recognition in some places. Again and again I discovered dark little spots in the sand between the footprints. Blood, undoubtedly.

Just as I reached Layla, she gathered up the hem of her robe and got down on her knees.

"The wind has almost destroyed the trail by now, unfortunately," she said to me instead of a greeting. "And various creatures of the desert, passing through here, have added to the damage. The smell of blood may have attracted them."

I was not surprised by her behavior. This was the Layla I already knew from our first two sets of murder cases. Almost fanatically concentrated, like a trained bloodhound.

She shook her head in frustration. "It's no use. This is where the trail actually ends, I'm afraid. But look!"

She pointed with her hand to the ground in front of our feet, where I could make out nothing but randomly blurred sand.

"These seem to be the footprints of another person," Layla said. "Possibly those of Timotheos's killer? But they are barely recognizable. Impossible to determine what footwear this person wore, or how large his feet might have been. I can't even tell if this phantom purposefully smudged his own prints, or just got lucky with the wind conditions. In any case, I couldn't say where the attacker came from. From the desert? Or from our midst after all?"

She rose, smoothing the folds of her robe. "Shall we return to the camp?" she asked me. A deep furrow had appeared on her youthful forehead.

I sent the guard ahead. In broad daylight, within sight of the camp, we were probably in no danger.

Then, as Layla and I trudged side by side through the sand, I filled her in on my conversations of the last few hours.

I hoped that she would ask questions, as was her way. That I could discuss my thoughts with her and she would give me new impulses. That she would point out to me what I might have overlooked or misinterpreted.

Things had long been awkward between Layla and me in matters of the heart, but when it came to cracking murderous puzzles, we complemented each other perfectly. At least, that had been my experience in the past.

Now, however, Layla did not spark a lively discussion with me, as I had expected, but seemed to sink into a somber meditation that she obviously didn't want to let me enter into.

I asked her several times to share her thoughts with me after all. "I can see that something is bothering you," I said.

But she merely shook her head.

"It's nothing, master," was all she had to say to me.

What on earth was she brewing up?

XVIII

Faustinius, as he had promised, provided a proper burial for his dead scribe. Timotheos's body was transported back to Alexandria, accompanied by two slaves who were to take care of the details of the burial.

Faustinius and the rest of us continued our journey, however. We sailed further upstream along the Nile toward Memphis, which was only a day's journey south of Heliopolis.

Nearby the pyramids were waiting for us, another stop on our Wonders of the World route, which Layla and Faustinius in particular were already impatiently awaiting. But first we wanted to devote ourselves to the sights that Memphis itself had to offer.

Memphis, once the glittering metropolis of the pharaohs, now counted perhaps forty thousand inhabitants, and was widely famous for one thing: its dead.

The embalmers' shops, which could be found here in almost unbelievable numbers, were in some cases large-scale operations in which twenty or thirty deceased people per day could be prepared for their final journey—according to a millennia-old Egyptian custom that plunged a large number of our servants into sheer horror: the dead were made into mummies.

The people of Memphis were proud of their trade. They not only earned their money with said death rites, they also made a real spectacle out of it for paying tourists like us.

We were able to visit a number of the pompous tombs, smaller pyramids and semi-subterranean labyrinths of the dead, and we even had the opportunity to personally witness a kind of show mummification.

A guide had advised us to see this spectacle, or rather a shrewd businessman, who also sold us copies of the Egyptian Book of the Dead. The latter was a kind of travel guide, which one absolutely needed if one wanted to be prepared for the last journey in life in the best possible way. The good man assured us of this with great persuasiveness.

As one can easily imagine, Capito was burning for this macabre manual and especially for the aforementioned demonstration of the embalmers.

His readers loved such things, as he let us know—not for the first time. So it was thanks to him that we finally witnessed a spectacle that was even more horrible to watch than the mere idea had sounded. Only Capito himself was at all enthusiastic about it.

Well, that wasn't quite true. Layla, too, followed every step of the disgusting ritual with great excitement. The rest of us—especially Alma—spent most of our time closing our eyes or turning away in disgust. Even I, who am truly not squeamish, lost my otherwise blessed appetite in the evening after the spectacle.

As a customer of the mummifiers, one could opt for the low-cost program—which meant that the human corpse was simply left to dry in the sun.

If one paid for a luxury funeral—the full pharaonic program, as Capito derisively called it—one received the treatment we witnessed at the paid show.

First, the brain of the deceased was removed with a long hook. And that through the nose! Likewise the entrails were taken out. Then the body, emptied in this way, was dehydrated in natron, after which he resembled a dried fish, it seemed to me. This process took forty days, then he was put in resin and anointing oil, wrapped with bandages and finally carried to the grave.

For the families of the deceased, there were spacious halls in the necropolis where they could gather for feasts with their dearly loved dead. We were also able to see some of these rooms with our own eyes.

As I said before, our cooks found few enthusiastic eaters among us that evening.

As macabre as our sightseeing program might have been, it did me good, though. I eagerly absorbed all the new knowledge and impressions, even the less stomach-friendly ones.

With that, I managed to leave behind the bloody death of the scribe and the gloomy thoughts that had befallen me because of Alma.

I had found an explanation for Timotheos's death that I could live with—and sleep peacefully: if I had my way, a blackmailer had been murdered by a thief.

This was a hideous matter, but not one that directly affected me. And certainly not one that I would allow to spoil my trip.

And I had—just as I'd suggested to Faustinius—assigned my Optimus to spy on Capito. Now I hoped that these efforts would soon be crowned with success. By now, I considered the blabbermouth I already detested so much capable of almost anything. That he should be a thief seemed almost compellingly logical to me.

In truth, he probably didn't sell as many books about his hair-raising adventures as he always liked to claim. And he didn't seem to come from a good, wealthy family either. He was traveling with only one slave—why hadn't that struck me as odd from the beginning? It should have been obvious that he financed his journeys in a dishonorable way. By stealing from his trusting travel companions!

Possibly his writings and his literary genius, which he used to flaunt so ostentatiously, were in truth invented altogether, only a pretext behind which he could hide his true craft—that of a thief and swindler.

Faustinius had the guard at his living and sleeping tents reinforced at all hours of the day and night. He did not want to be robbed, that was only too understandable, but perhaps there was more behind it. Did he also fear for his life?

Nevertheless, my old friend showed himself in high spirits toward me and the others, as we dined and drank and enjoyed the wonders of Memphis to the fullest.

As usual, we had set up our camp a little outside the city, once again between the fertile banks of the Nile and the dunes of the desert.

On the third morning of our stay, I was walking past Alma's tent when I witnessed a strange incident: the beautiful and otherwise gentle Northerner threw her faithful slave out of the tent. And she did so with loud imprecations.

"Get out of my sight, you old harpy," she scolded the faithful Zenobia.

I could not believe my ears. That was hardly the tone of voice I was used to from Alma.

Zenobia ran away crying bitterly, while Alma froze to a pillar of salt when she discovered me. She was visibly embarrassed that I had witnessed her outburst of anger.

I walked up to her with a questioning look.

Since Timotheos had died, Alma's interest, indeed, her entire attention, had been unreservedly on me, and I must confess to my shame that I liked that very much.

I had not hated Timotheos, although he had been my rival in Alma's favor. The scribe had been a clever and honorable fellow, at least that's what I had assumed for the longest time. Even if he'd been quite arrogant.

By finally revealing to me the rapacious motives behind his courtship of Alma he had rather clouded that picture. And the fact that he had then also betrayed his master and proposed a horse trade to a sneaky thief made his murder at least understandable—even though I had of course not wanted his death for a moment.

I was tormented now and then by a guilty conscience that, thanks to his sudden demise, I had Alma's affection all to myself again—an affection that she barely tried to hide from me any longer. Indeed, I was quite sure that she had true and deep feelings for me.

Now, however, I seemed to have a woman in front of me whom I had not yet met up to that point.

Alma hid her face in her hands and was breathing heavily. "Forgive me, Thanar, what must you think of me now! But Zenobia can be really impossible sometimes," she moaned.

I gently put my arm around her shoulders, enjoying her

leaning against me as a matter of course.

"What happened?" I asked. "Was she guilty of something?" I would have been very surprised.

Alma hunched her shoulders.

"Not really. It's just ... oh, I'm sure she means well, but sometimes her care crushes me. I sent her away, told her to sleep with the other slaves from now on and stop clinging to me all the time. I don't need a yard dog lurking at my doorstep, fearfully eyeing my every move."

Of course, she wasn't telling me anything new with that. I had long noticed her slave's clingy behavior myself.

"So it's that bad?" I asked, but more rhetorically than in wonder.

Alma nodded.

"Not even my nursemaid was so concerned about me!" she cried heatedly. "Zenobia is constantly pestering me that we should finally go home. To Rome—where I don't feel at home at all. She is such a fearful and superstitious creature, seeing dark omens everywhere, and all the wonders of our journey seem to mean nothing to her. She is convinced that I am in constant danger, that something could happen to me. That I might fall ill and she might lose me. That the gods of Egypt are angry with me. I don't know. She also cannot be dissuaded from the belief that poor Timotheos fell victim to a demon. And that all of us, our entire group of friends, are no longer safe here."

"I would never let anything happen to you," I said gallantly, pulling her tighter against me.

Alma raised her head and smiled at me.

"I do feel completely safe by your side, Thanar," she said, "and I don't want to have our trip spoiled! I'm enjoying it so much. Hah, already I can't wait until we finally see the pyramids!"

XIX

On the fourth evening of our stay in Memphis, I fell onto my bed, dead tired. The day had brought a whole wealth of new experiences, and Alma had not left my side for a moment.

Together we had visited the mighty temple of Ptah and the sanctuary of the Apis Bull. As I have already mentioned, it is a peculiarity of the Egyptians to worship various animals as deities. Among them can also be found this holy bovine. Through a small window we were allowed to take a look into the stables of the Memphis bull and watch him during his afternoon walk in the courtyard of the temple.

But at the end of the day, I was not to enjoy my high spirits any longer. The gods had other plans for us, terrible plans. In some way we must have enraged them anew.

In the middle of the night I was jolted out of sleep by panicked screaming. I thought at first that my nightmares had returned, but that was not the case. The screaming came from beyond my tent.

Dazed, I dressed and staggered out into the open. There was a commotion in the camp, and here again, it seemed to me for a moment as if I had to relive that night of Timotheos' terrible death.

In truth, however, the sight that presented itself to me was many times worse. Two slaves, who seemed to have made their return from the desert and appeared to be completely drunk, were just dragging a third fellow back into the camp. The man's arms and bare chest were covered in bloody wounds.

He was barely able to stand on his feet, and he was screaming like a man possessed and flailing his arms. He and the other two fellows had come shuffling out of the desert's darkness like hungry demons.

I hurried towards them—together with some slaves who were running from their own sleeping place. The terrible screaming must have roused them as well. They looked around fearfully and pressed close together. Certainly they believed themselves to be under the curse of the Pharaohs again.

I reached the three fellows dragging themselves from the desert, pushed one aside, and helped the badly wounded man make the last steps into camp.

To my horror, I realized that the wounded lad was Lurco, Faustinius's beautiful boy-toy and barber.

There was hardly anything left of the usually well-groomed lad's everyday appearance. His long hair hung straggling into his forehead, he was bleeding from several wounds, and his gaze resembled that of a madman.

"Anubis," he gasped, "he came upon me, full of wrath! He threatened my life!"

He looked around in a hurry, which seemed to cause him new pain.

"We are all doomed to die," he moaned. "Our fate is sealed."

With these words he collapsed. I was just able to catch him and soften his fall somewhat.

The two fellows who had dragged him into camp were

hardly in a better condition. They too fell to the ground, crying for water and howling that the god of the dead was personally claiming their lives.

However, I could not make out any serious injuries on their bodies. Apart from a few scratches, they seemed unharmed. The blood that was on their hands seemed to be Lurco's, not their own.

I looked around for Optimus. Apart from Lurco, these men belonged to my guard. But where was their leader? He couldn't possibly have slept through this commotion?

By now, all the members of our tour group seemed to be on their feet. Men and women, slaves, servants and guards came rushing toward me, some of them insufficiently clothed. They were all coming to the aid of the wounded man.

Faustinius made his way between them a moment later, hurried toward me, and fell to his knees beside his barber.

In the meantime, I had put Lurco on a blanket, but he did not stop howling and wailing. He was certainly in pain, but it seemed to me that above all his mind was filled with sheer horror. He must have seen something unspeakable out there in the desert.

Faustinius looked at the whimpering wretch for a brief moment, then pulled at his own hair with an agonized groan and barked orders at his other slaves to help the barber.

In a hopeless confusion, the slaves were running about in the camp. Hardly any of them seemed to be in their right mind.

"Those were the djinn of the desert!" a voice called out. "They have come to take us. We are not welcome here in the holy places of the Pharaohs!"

The djinn were dark demons who were said to dwell in the endless steppes and among the dunes. Another belief of the Egyptians—which our slaves had adopted only too willingly.

"It is the undead who are pursuing us. They have crawled out of their graves and want our blood!" cried another. "They curse us because we have disturbed their peace!"

This was not the first time I had heard this accusation. The fact that we visited the necropolis of Memphis had caused incomprehension, if not sheer horror, among many of the servants.

"It was Anubis himself who attacked Lurco," gasped one of the two guards who had just dragged the wounded barber into camp. "I saw him with my own eyes. He pounced on Lurco, and only with much yelling were we able to chase him away! By a hair we would all have been doomed to death!"

"The curse from the Pharaohs," howled a shrill female voice. "Did I warn you not all about it?" Judging from her broken Latin, it was a kitchen maid or similar low-ranking slave.

At that moment, another figure emerged from the darkness surrounding the camp. It was one of the guard slaves who belonged to Alma's familia, a dark-haired Gaul, normally almost as imperturbable as my Optimus. He came shuffling into the camp, silent and limping badly. No word escaped his lips, but his gaze was filled with nameless fear.

What had happened to these men?

I am usually quite a sober person, not easily scared by

dark magic or the old wives' tales of slaves. But something must have happened to these men that exceeded any earthly horror.

A few helpers rushed toward the guard. They were those among the slaves who still seemed the least frightened. The Gaul leaned heavily on the helping arms and went staggering to the ground when he had safely reached the camp. He looked around as if he hardly recognized the familiar place.

He also made the impression on me that he had indulged in a true orgy of Bacchus; had he and the other men got drunk beyond all measure—only to run out into the desert? Where they'd met Anubis himself?

None of this made the slightest sense.

XX

The Gaul was led to the campfire. He was given water and wrapped in a blanket. However, he did not seem to be physically injured.

Behind me, Faustinius suddenly howled aloud.

I whirled around—and froze at the sight before me.

My friend held his barber in his arms, squeezed him, shook him, lovingly stroked a strand of hair from his forehead, kissed his cheeks. But then he lowered him to the ground and began to cry bitterly.

Lurco had lost his battle with death. The life had run out of his beautiful young limbs. Like a limp doll, he lay before the knees of his wailing master.

I saw a slender, dark female figure detach herself from the crowd, walk up to Faustinius, and lean down to him.

It was Layla.

She whispered some words to my friend that I could not understand. She was certainly trying to soothe the pain of his loss and to give him comfort. But I also noticed that at the same time she was looking at the barber's corpse with a scrutinizing gaze.

Finally, she turned her full attention to the dead man. She ran her fingertips over some of the wounds gaping on Lurco's arms and hairless chest. It looked like she was trying to trace them. Not exactly a moral thing for a woman to do, but with Layla it didn't really surprise. I knew that she didn't see a man in front of her in the corpse, who might have been attractive when he was alive, but merely a bloody new mystery that needed to be solved.

Nevertheless, she did not lack compassion—neither for the dead, nor for Faustinius, his master, who was clearly so deeply affected by the loss. Again and again, she exchanged a few whispered words with my grieving friend, and touched the corpse only with extreme caution— obviously anxious not to disturb his resting place.

Next, she bent close over the barber's face.

What was she doing? It seemed as if she was sniffing his lips. Indeed, in the next moment she even opened them gently with her fingertips, and then once again took in the air through her nose. Finally, she stared intently for quite a while into the dead man's eyes, which were already directing their broken gaze into the beyond.

I summoned some of my men—those who were not looking like the living dead themselves—and sent them out to look for Optimus.

"Take torches and swords and fan out," I ordered. "He must be out there somewhere, or he'd be with us by now. But stay together in groups of two. And take care!"

I silently implored the gods that my faithful Optimus had not met a fate similar to that of Faustinius's barber. Then I hurried to Layla's side; she had just risen from the ground. Her examination seemed to be completed.

She looked at me thoughtfully, although I was not sure whether she was aware of me at all. Her thoughts were visibly circling around Lurco's demise.

I took her aside while Faustinius also rose and had his lifeless slave carried away. He gave instructions to lay Lurco out, wash and anoint him. I was sure that the dead barber would be given far more extensive funeral rites than Timotheos the scribe. Perhaps even a pharaonic program right here in Memphis?

Some slave girls sang a lament for Lurco, the others went their way with hanging heads. The young barber had clearly been very popular, what with his friendly and humorous nature.

"What do you think happened to Lurco?" I asked, turning to Layla when I thought we were safely out of earshot. "Or rather, what happened to all those men? They strike me as having indulged in an insane drinking binge ... and then they must have just wandered off into the desert...?"

That couldn't possibly be the case.

Well, not every slave or servant was a model of discipline and reliability, and indulging in the pleasures of Bacchus during the night hours, when their masters were asleep, was one of the few pleasures open to them on this journey. For such as this they could not be blamed.

But that several of them had drunk themselves into a half-mad frenzy? I couldn't believe that by any stretch of the imagination.

Layla swayed her head back and forth.

"There was a strange, foamy coating on Lurco's tongue," she explained in a matter-of-fact tone. "Like that found in people afflicted with raving madness. But his wounds, most of them anyway ... they could actually have come from an animal. The men claim to have seen Anubis, don't they?"

I nodded. "But I hope you're not trying to make me

believe that the dog-headed god himself was after Lurco's life."

As far as I knew, the Egyptians worshiped Anubis as the lord and judge of the dead, who also watched over the funeral rites—over the embalming, mummification and burial—and the safe escort of the departed souls into the world of the beyond. Surely the slaves had now come to believe that the dog-headed god was pursuing us as intruders because we had desecrated the holy peace of the Necropolis with our sightseeing.

But I was certainly not ready to accept this gloomy superstition!

Neither, thankfully, did Layla. "No," she said, "I rather think the men encountered hyenas or jackals in the desert."

That was much easier for me to accept. We had come across these strange beasts several times already on our route through Egypt. We had spotted them in the distance, and often heard their howling or barking at night. But these creatures were quite small and shy. I could not imagine that they would attack a human being—or even several—and bite them to death.

"I didn't look at Lurco's wounds up close like you did," I said, "but those on his chest seemed like cuts or puncture wounds, didn't they? They were too smooth and regular for the claws or even the teeth of a predator."

Layla nodded. "That's what I thought, too. But there also were lots of bite and scratch marks on his body"

"Then I can guess what may have happened to him," I said. "He was attacked—neither by an animal, nor by a mummy, and certainly not by Anubis himself. But by a human adversary with a knife or a sword. Perhaps the attacker was intent on making his assault look like an animal attack, and deliberately inflicted only minor cuts on Lurco. But then he trusted that the predators of the desert would smell the blood—and see the weakened victim as easy prey. The comrades who found Lurco half-dead then probably saw jackals or hyenas approaching their friend, or even already feasting on him."

Layla nodded. "But what drove Lurco into the desert? And the other men. They—"

Layla didn't get any further, because at that moment fresh screams rang out.

I turned my head, startled, and saw that a new commotion had broken out at the other end of the camp. A few of the men I had sent out to look for Optimus appeared among the barrels of supplies that were stored over there.

They staggered along, bent under a heavy load they were carrying between them, calling attention to themselves with loud shouts. Some slaves rushed to their aid.

I myself immediately jumped up and also crossed the camp as fast as my legs could carry me.

To my horror, I realized that it was a man the fellows were dragging. One whose figure was all too familiar to me by now.

"Optimus!" I cried and rushed to his side. Yes, no doubt about it, it was my faithful veteran!

He groaned as the men laid him down on a quickly brought blanket. He looked as dazed and confused as Lurco and the others had before.

But he certainly hadn't drunk himself into a stupor and

lost control. Not my Optimus. Never!

"Lions," he breathed. "Horrible beasts."

He had never been a man of many words. He gritted his teeth and put on a brave smile. He looked badly battered, as if he had taken on half a dozen opponents.

His face was scuffed, his lips completely parched, but a slave was already hurrying over with a damp cloth and a large cup of water.

Optimus eagerly reached for the cup, but his fingers missed by a good hand's width. His eyelids flickered.

I supported him with my hand on the back of his neck and helped him bring the cup to his mouth with the other. He drank like a man dying of thirst.

Layla appeared next to me. At the sight of the brave guard, she slapped her hands together in front of her face. Even she, who was usually so hardened, was shocked by the sight of him.

When Optimus had emptied the water cup, I stood up, leaving the slaves to patch up my faithful guard.

He was well cared for, and one look at his wounds told me that his life was not in danger, as hideous as the injuries might look. They weren't deep, just misshapen and blood-crusted, a myriad of scrapes and bites. They had to hurt like hell, but Optimus would not succumb to them.

Layla also intently examined the injuries on his body.

"These do look like a predator's marks to me. *Exclusively* a predator's," I told her. "They're very different injuries than the ones we saw on Lurco."

She nodded. "In his case, I don't think anyone has done any preliminary damage with a knife."

"Let Optimus get some rest and regain his strength," I said, "then hopefully he can tell us what happened to him and to the other men."

XXI

Layla and I directed our steps to the campfire to warm up a bit, and settled there.

I started pondering.

"Do you think," I said to my black Sphinx after a while, "that Lurco was lured into the desert and attacked there? Like Timotheos before him?"

"That's what it looks like, at least at second glance," she replied. It was one of her typically cryptic answers, after which one had more questions than before.

"Lurco must have managed to call for help," I continued, "and the guards from the camp rushed to his side. But then what became of the attacker? I can't imagine that a mere mortal could overpower several of our men, including Optimus to boot."

Layla gave me a questioning look. "No mere mortal?" she murmured.

"That's nonsense, of course," I quickly replied. "It *must* have been someone mortal. But you truly can't blame the simpler minds among us for thinking sorcerers or demons are at work here!"

Layla nodded slowly. "Optimus spoke of lions, the other men spoke of Anubis..."

"Whereby we suspected hyenas or jackals," I interjected. "And a human with a sharp blade! But what confused and frightened the men so? I just don't understand it."

The report that Optimus finally gave us on the evening of the same day, when he had regained his strength, made little more sense than the ghost stories of our frightened slaves.

"We were sitting around the fire," he began, "as we do every evening after the masters have gone to sleep. At first there were about twenty of us—slaves, servants, guards— then more and more people withdrew. In the end, there were maybe six or seven of us left, and suddenly the night seemed to come to life. The darkness that surrounded us became phantoms, horrible demons, screeching wildly. Sounds of madness, sir, if ever I heard any! And a stench as if we were being roasted alive. My stomach churned."

He faltered and rubbed his temples with erratic movements.

"I know how this sounds," he continued hesitantly, "but I really think that a dark spell came over us. The curse of the pharaohs, sir! It was a mistake not to take it seriously!"

"Come on, Optimus," I said, "don't you start that too, please!"

He raised his hands imploringly. "But it is the truth, sir! If you had experienced what happened to me last night ... if you had seen what I saw with my own eyes, you would believe me! I beheld ... oh, by Jupiter, I have no idea what it really was! How can I describe it? It was shadows, chimeras, spirits rising before my eyes, attacking me. And my comrades felt the same way."

Such words, from the mouth of my usually sober veteran? I could not believe my ears. A dark, paralyzing cold started spreading in my stomach.

"And then what happened?" I asked. "Were you attacked? Didn't you mention lions?"

Optimus nodded with a somber look. "The lions, yes ... but they came much later. Hours later, I think. When the ghosts had long since finished with us and left us more dead than alive. I tell you, they pounced on us like the Furies, those night creatures! With horrible screams and grimaces that made my blood run cold—"

Again he interrupted himself. "I honestly don't think I'm a coward, Thanar...."

"Of course not," I said quickly. "No one doubts your courage."

"And yet I was seized with sheer terror. I ran. Ran as fast as my legs would carry me. Just like my comrades."

"You escaped into the desert?" I asked.

"I don't remember that. I just fled, as far away as possible."

"And then what happened?"

Optimus shrugged his muscular shoulders. "I have no idea. It is as if the hours that followed have been erased from my memory. When I regained half my senses, I found myself facing a hungry pride of lions. I was just able to fend them off, even though they probably saw a right tidbit in me. Fortunately, my sword was still on my belt. The demons had probably left it to me, because they did not need to fear my blade. I could not harm them with it. But the hairy leonine beasts disliked it very much!"

He gave a pained smile. Beads of sweat stood on his forehead, which he tried to wipe away with a nervous movement of his hand.

"Then I spied a glow of light on the horizon," he

continued. "The torches and lamps here in the camp. I mustered the last of my strength, and dragged myself toward them. But I was not myself! I could not feel my legs as I ran, and still ghastly figures were pursuing me."

"And what happened to Lurco?" I asked. "He was sitting with you by the fire, I suppose?"

"He was. I remember that much. But after that...."

Optimus shook his head. "I wish I knew, sir. Surely he too became a victim of the demons."

"He was wounded with a sword, my good Optimus," I contradicted him.

"Yes ... that's what I was told."

He hunched his shoulders and looked at me, perplexed.

"Could it be that you ... well, drank a few cups too many, last night?" I asked—albeit reluctantly.

The look Optimus gave me in reply pained me. I had hurt his honor, just as I had expected.

"How can you think that of me, Thanar?" he said in a strained voice. "No, I swear to you, none of us guards drank more than the usual cup or two. A few of the slaves perhaps got a little carried away, but they had long since gone to bed when these spooky creatures attacked us."

"Are you sure it couldn't have been flesh and blood men who attacked you?" I dug deeper. "In strange disguise, perhaps, to hoodwink you?" I was not yet ready to believe in an attack by demons, even though I had to admit that not much was missing to convince me.

Optimus shook his head vigorously. The next moment he groaned in agony. His hands went to his temples. A new pain must have shot through him.

I couldn't help but be reminded of a hangover the

morning after a drinking binge.

"It wasn't disguises I saw!" Optimus cried. "But the living dead and creatures of the night! With rotting limbs, maggots crawling from their eye sockets, and a stench of burnt flesh. Others had eyes that blazed like fire, black wings, razor-sharp claws. If this was a disguise—no, never."

"You were sitting around the fire, you said," Layla suddenly chimed in. "When you were ambushed?"

Optimus nodded. "Yes ... why?"

She stood up, smoothed her tunic with a few strokes of her hand, and walked over to the fireplace that formed the center of the servants' area. Optimus and I gave each other an uncomprehending look—then we followed her.

Layla knelt down next to the soot-blackened hollow, which was bordered by stones. At the moment, only some embers were glowing in it.

She looked back at me. "Your knife, Thanar. May I borrow it for a moment?"

I reached for my belt, unsheathed my sax, and handed it to Layla.

She began to poke around in the ashes with it, bending so low over the embers that I was afraid she might scorch her hair. Then, with a highly concentrated gaze, she started to examine every tiny piece of charred wood she found in the hollow. With the help of my short sword, she rummaged through the entire fire pit in this way.

Finally, she rose and turned to Optimus. "Can you remember if the fire produced much smoke last night— just before the demons attacked you?"

What a strange question.

Optimus frowned. "Now that you ask me that, yes, I think it did. We thought we had gotten some badly dried logs. And together with the demons a dark mist came over us."

"And a terrible stench, right?" added Layla. "You said earlier that the phantoms who attacked you were spreading it."

"That's right," Optimus said.

He looked at Layla with a questioning look, not seeming to grasp what she was getting at.

Neither did I.

Layla got down on her knees again, turned back to the fire pit, and kept poking.

The next moment she gave a sharp cry of triumph. I could see that she was pushing a very small, badly charred piece of wood out of the embers. With the help of the knife tip, she managed to do so without burning her fingers.

"Look here," she said, pointing her head at the tiny black piece.

I squinted my eyes, got down on my knees as well—and realized that it wasn't wood at all. It was slightly curved, and looked like... "A claw?" I asked.

Layla shook her head.

She blew over the find a few times, then carefully lifted it with her fingers and placed it on her open palm.

Optimus and I bent over it at the same time.

"The sting of a scorpion!" Layla announced. "I'm sure several of them were thrown into the flames last night, but most of them have probably already been reduced to ash or swept away when the fireplace was cleaned."

"And that signifies what?" asked Optimus,

uncomprehending.

Layla looked thoughtfully into his eyes. "It signifies that a human meant you harm. Not a demon."

"But—" Optimus wanted to protest.

Layla wouldn't let him get a word in edgewise, though. "A human who made use of a scorpion," she added. "Or rather, a small army of scorpions."

XXII

Optimus stared at her as if she had lost her mind. And I have to admit that I couldn't figure out what Layla was getting at either. But I was used to the fact that my black Sphinx often talked in riddles, since I knew her much better than my unfortunate veteran did.

"Surely you've seen them before, these black, well-armored creatures," she continued, addressing Optimus. "They are native here, just as they were in my former homeland. That's how I know them, and—"

"I know what a scorpion is," Optimus interrupted her. "But the sting in the fire pit...?"

"The sting of this vermin can be fatal," Layla explained, "but only in the case of a few species. Most are pretty harmless. But if you smoke the poison of their sting instead of putting it into your blood ... it can open the portals. To the realm of the gods, but also to that of the demons. Among the men of my people, it was a popular ritual to smoke scorpion stingers."

I finally understood what Layla was getting at with her story. "Then someone captured some of those scorpions," I concluded, "stripped them of their stingers, and threw those into the fire last night? And it was the smoke that drove the men mad?"

"I think that's exactly what happened," Layla said. "It must have been someone sitting by the fire with you," she said, turning to Optimus again. "Or someone who could approach you without arousing suspicion. Throwing a handful of those tiny things into the flames in the dark, not necessarily all at the same time ... it wouldn't be very noticeable, I guess."

Optimus puckered up his face.

"What a diabolical plan," he grumbled, "but you're right, Layla. We were chatting and laughing ... we were among friends. None of us kept his or her eyes on the fire like a treasure to be guarded."

Layla nodded in understanding.

"The vile demons," she said, "whom you described to us, who attacked you and drove you into the desert, were mere mirages from the realm of shadows. Not opponents in the flesh. The poison of the scorpions made you have nightmares with your eyes open. *That's* what you fled from."

A hint of shame flitted across the veteran's features. The idea that he had let himself be thrown into such a panic by mere shadow images did not please him at all. That was clearly visible to me.

"It must have been as Layla says," I took the floor. "You reported, my dear Optimus, that the undead and demons you saw let out terrible screams when they attacked you. Didn't they?"

He nodded uncertainly.

"Just think," I said, "if that had really happened, that infernal noise would have roused everyone here in the camp from their sleep, wouldn't it? So it could only have been an illusion."

"Then I just heard the screaming in my head?" grumbled Optimus.

"I'm afraid so," I said.

The veteran's gaze traveled down his arms, where several bandages sat. "But the lions ... they were not mirages," he said. "I assure you of that!"

I nodded. "And neither was the knife that made Lurco bleed," I added.

"He alone was injured in that particular way, wasn't he?" asked Layla. "Five men—including you, Optimus—ran out into the desert, but only Lurco suffered those injuries."

"I had a look at his corpse earlier," Optimus replied. "And if you ask me, whoever inflicted those wounds on him and thought they'd pass for bites or scratches ... well, they probably don't know much about combat wounds."

Or that's what they wanted us to believe, it suddenly flashed through my mind.

"Perhaps the attacker had only a short time available for his bloody deed," I suggested. "Maybe Lurco took flight or tried to fight back?"

Optimus shook his head. "If he had defended himself, there should be more cuts on his hands and forearms."

He raised his arms in a protective gesture to illustrate his words. "But that was not the case," he added.

"Anyway, the attacker injured Lurco badly enough," I said, "and then probably counted on the predators of the desert to find the bleeding and severely weakened victim and finish him off. And as far as we can say, that is just how it happened."

"A targeted and cold-blooded murder, then, do you think?" said Optimus, an expression of disgust settling over his angular features.

I nodded. "Even though we can't prove it, of course."

"But why Lurco?" Optimus objected. "A completely harmless fellow who would have never hurt a fly. Who would want to harm such a person?"

"Why did Timotheos have to die?" I replied. "We don't know that either."

Optimus raised both eyebrows in wonder. "You think the two deaths are connected?"

Again, I nodded. "It's possible. Maybe Lurco had to die because he knew something about the first murder? Maybe he had overheard a telltale conversation or even witnessed the crime itself?"

A thought forced its way into my head. One that filled me with excitement.

I looked first at Optimus, then at Layla. "Faustinius claimed that Lurco occasionally used to walk in his sleep, remember? That's what he gave as the reason why you found the barber in the corridor at a late hour, Optimus. Back in Alexandria, in the house of Petronius, close to Alma's room, where Lurco had really no business being."

The veteran nodded.

"Well ... what if that was actually true?" I continued. Even though I myself hadn't wanted to believe this explanation at the time, as I still remembered well. "Perhaps on the night when Timotheos died, Lurco was again overcome by this nocturnal wandering habit—and happened to run into the scribe's murderer? Faustinius did claim that Lurco was unaware of his surroundings during these nocturnal excursions—but this time he may have woken up. Perhaps because his body sensed danger, even if his mind was not initially alert. Then Lurco may have witnessed what happened to Timotheos, or at least been able to observe who followed the scribe out into the desert."

Optimus gave me a strange look. "It seems to me you have some experience with such bloody deeds—with murders? Forgive me for saying so, sir," he added quickly.

"That's all right," I responded sullenly. "You're correct, I'm afraid, though I truly don't want to boast of these experiences. I wish the gods would line my path with harmony and joy ... instead of one corpse after another."

I looked over at Layla, who had been standing next to us for a while, silent and seemingly lost in thought, motionless as a statue.

What was going on in her head? I was certain I wouldn't know until she was ready to tell me, so I didn't even attempt to question her.

Instead, I turned to Optimus again. "Please try to remember: who was sitting with you by the fire, or came by, just before the mirages started overwhelming you? Lurco and the other men who ran out into the desert, I suppose? But who else?"

I'd already had a conversation with the two slaves who had found Lurco and dragged him back to camp. They had hardly been able to remember anything. They, too, had told me a wild story about djinn, undead, and the vengeful spirits of the pharaohs who had pursued them. And that sometime later, in the middle of the desert, they had come to with nothing but confused memories. The cries of a seriously injured man—Lurco—had startled them out of a dull sleep, and they had risen to help him.

"A few slave girls were still sitting with us," Optimus said after thinking for a while. "In the beginning, anyway. I don't remember when they left us. I think it was Anna, Mirabila and Zenobia. The former two are maidservants of Faustinius," he added.

I nodded. The two girls were familiar to me. At least I knew their names.

The forehead of my troubled veteran was deeply wrinkled. He was visibly struggling to wring as many impressions as possible from his memory—and seemed to hate himself for not succeeding better.

"Then there were two coachmen," he continued, "also servants of Faustinius ... but I also saw some of the gentlemen. They weren't sitting by the fire with us, but they came by. I'm positive I saw Capito. He addressed one of the slaves, who then jumped up and followed him. Otherwise ... oh, I don't remember. The memories are so hazy, as if it all happened months ago."

Layla found her tongue again. "Let's question Zenobia, Thanar," she said abruptly. "Perhaps she was able to observe something that would help us?"

We left Optimus behind. I told him to get plenty of sleep tonight. In the meantime, others could take over his guard duty. We went in search of Alma's body slave.

We found Zenobia where we thought she would be: in her mistress's tent. She was helping Alma fix her hair for dinner.

The slave willingly gave information, even if the events of the previous night had also taken their toll on her.

"Poor Lurco," she kept sobbing until we finally managed to calm her down a bit and elicit a semi-understandable report from her.

"Yes," she confirmed, sniffling, "we sat together for a long time last night. Many of us who had no vigil to keep, and could have gone to sleep, stayed by the fire anyway. Longer than usual, sir. Being so close to this city of the dead, many of us were afraid to shut our eyes, lest we never open them again!"

She faltered, seeming to lose herself in dark visions.

"Go ahead," I urged her. "What happened next?"

"Next?" she repeated dreamily.

She swallowed, tightening her shoulders. "At some point we were eventually overcome by fatigue," she continued haltingly. "I think I was one of the last women still sitting by the fire with the men. Then, however, I got up to check on my mistress. I wondered if she needed anything before I went to sleep."

She gave Alma an almost tender look.

"Just before you left the campfire," I asked, "did you notice anything unusual? Thicker smoke from the fire, perhaps? An unusual smell? Did you see demons or other creatures of the night?"

Zenobia shook her head. "No, sir. I was just a bit surprised later when I returned and found the fireplace completely deserted. But of course it was none of my business how the guards did their work," she added quickly.

"Why did you return to the fire again?" interjected Layla. "Didn't you want to go to sleep?"

"I was looking for my mistress," Zenobia replied. "As I said, I wanted to see if she still needed me. But I couldn't find her in her tent. So I walked through the camp again to look for her. In the end, I also went over to the servants' area. I thought that maybe she'd be looking for me there, because she needed something—and we had just missed each other. The camp is quite large, isn't it?"

Again, her gaze sought Alma's.

"I was worried about you," she addressed her mistress directly. "But then I found you in your tent when I hurried back here again. You had returned in the meantime and were already sleeping peacefully. So I could then go to bed with a light heart."

She nodded her head as if to emphasize her own words. Then she humbly narrowed her eyes.

Alma, however, frowned. "You were looking for me, you say? Impossible—I was here in my tent the whole time. I had lain down very early."

She gave me a warm look. "Our days, my dear Thanar, are so full of the most wonderful impressions that I usually fall into bed at night completely exhausted," she explained to me with a subtle smile.

Zenobia looked at her mistress uncomprehendingly. "But I—" she began, then seemed to remember her position, not wanting to contradict.

She lowered her eyes and pulled in her shoulders.

"Then I must have been mistaken," she whispered, "Forgive me, mistress."

XXIII

The pyramids turned out to be more magnificent than any structure I could have ever imagined. Like the sacred mountains of Olympus, they rose into the sky before us. The white stone with which they were clad shone so brilliantly in the sun that we had to close our eyes.

There were three pyramids rising on a rocky plateau—and next to them a Sphinx of equally imposing size.

Even more so than at the other stops on our great journey, we were beset here by merchants, guides, portrait painters, astrologers, and sorcerers, who offered their services to us as soon as we disembarked from our Nile ship.

The guide we finally hired was a priest who greeted us at the Pharaohs' burial temple. From this sage we learned miraculous things:

"You think the pyramids you see are huge?" he began in a nasal scholarly tone that made me think of our chatty Capito. "But know that in truth they are even more enormous! For they extend as deep under the earth as their tops reach into the sky! And do you want to know how they were erected? How it was possible to move and place the two million blocks that were laid here, each of them weighing thousands of pounds?"

Of course we wanted to know. The question literally forced itself on you when you stood in amazement in front of this wonder of the world.

The guide smiled. "They were not just masters of their trade, the builders of the ancient pharaohs!" he announced, "but also shrewd and clever! They built mountains of salt around the construction site, as ramps for the blocks. And then, when the job was done, they used the waters of the Nile to melt away the makeshift building works!"

Layla, who was walking next to me, gave me a skeptical look but said nothing.

Our guide also told us about the enormous sums of money that had gone into the building of the pyramids. During the construction of the second pyramid, none other than the daughter of the pharaoh had opened a brothel, he claimed, where she'd offered herself also to the highest bidders, thereby helping to finance the glorious building.

"And while we are on the subject of venal love," the guide added in a theatrical tone, "know that in the third and smallest pyramid lies buried a Greek hetaera! The mistress of the poet Aesop she is said to have been, but then the Pharaoh himself fell in love with her and built her this tomb for eternity."

Despite these incredible—and saucy—details, our guide's words hardly seemed to reach my friend Faustinius. He listened to the explanations as eagerly and patiently as was his way, but I could tell that they meant little to him.

He sat languidly in his carrying chair, shoulders drooping, lost in mourning thoughts of Lurco. Often, when our guide fell silent, he murmured the name of the dead barber to himself, as if he were still in a living conversation with his lost one.

The rest of us, Layla, Alma and myself, tried our best to comfort him, but none of us really managed to succeed.

Capito, never at a loss for a suitable anecdote, began to tell of how the Emperor Hadrianus, when he himself had traveled through Egypt a few years ago, had had to endure a similarly painful loss. Death did not stop even before the greatest!

Hadrianus had been traveling with his favorite slave, Antinoos. A gentle youth, very similar to Faustinius's Lurco, as Capito pointed out. But one day the lifeless body of the beautiful boy was pulled out of the Nile. He had drowned, and the emperor's heart was broken.

"Rumor has it Empress Sabina, inflamed with jealousy, may have had a hand in it," Capito added, clicking his tongue whimsically.

When we were already on the way back to our camp after this first inspection of the pyramids, and Faustinius was just out of earshot, Capito told one of his beloved jokes. He probably thought it was particularly appropriate.

A man comes to Elithios Phoitetes and complains, "This slave you sold me a few days ago has just died."

To which Elithios replies, "That amazes me. In all the time he was with me, he never did anything like that!"

Layla was also in a strangely melancholy mood that evening. As we sat together at sunset, the massive pyramids well in view, she lost herself in somber reflections.

"They seem so huge, so imperishable," she began, with a

jerky hand gesture toward the monuments. "Do you think that one day they will crumble just like the walls of Babylon?"

I looked at her in surprise. I knew Layla as a true ray of sunshine—always in a good mood and positive.

"For the life of me, I can't imagine what would destroy those pyramids," I answered her. "But time brings changes to all things; it always has. Some changes are enjoyable, others ... well, are less pleasant."

I really didn't have what it takes to be a philosopher. In this respect, I had never deluded myself.

Layla looked at me intently. The warm light of the evening was reflected in her dark eyes.

"Do you think that even the almighty Empire will one day perish?" she continued her somber meditations.

"Really, dear," I addressed her with my old tenderness, "now you are carrying things too far! What power on earth could ever overthrow eternal Rome?"

She shrugged apologetically, and at last a small smile started playing around the corners of her mouth.

"And as for the mortality of us all," I added, "perhaps we must arm ourselves with bitter humor? For once, along the lines of Capito, the pain in the ass?"

Layla's smile widened, but it did not reach her eyes. They remained serious and watchful, even though I had the impression that they were looking right through me. Something was on Layla's mind, I would wager—apart from general questions about the transience of all human endeavor.

"Capito is more skilled than I would have given him credit for, though," I continued, trying to distract her a bit.

"He may be a show-off and torment us with silly jokes—but if he really is a thief, he knows his way around the trade."

Layla did not respond.

I could have sworn that I could distract her with such a topic. She loved to uncover criminal machinations, to bring villains to justice. What was wrong with her?

I nodded to emphasize my words, but even that had no visible effect.

"I put my Optimus to spy on Capito, remember?" I said then. "So far, though, my good veteran hasn't been able to accuse our chatterbox of anything—at least regarding the thefts Faustinius was talking about. Do you think that in the end he has wronged Capito with this accusation?"

Layla hardly seemed to follow my words. "It's something else that gives me food for thought," she said abruptly.

XXIV

"I just remembered something I had completely forgotten," Layla explained to me abruptly. "Or rather, it didn't seem to have any particular meaning to me at the time it occurred."

"Once again you speak in riddles, my dear," I replied.

At least with this remark I could elicit a slight brightening of her beautiful features. Layla loved to play the inscrutable, the mysterious. She would never have admitted that, but I knew it!

"It's about a conversation I had with Capito," she continued. "Or rather, one he had with me. It was on the ship, days before we went ashore in Alexandria."

"And what was it about?"

She frowned. "Capito spoke to me about my homeland. He asked me about the customs and everyday life of my people—which didn't surprise me at all. He may be a talker and spice his stories with the craziest lies, but he is also an eager collector of information. Of knowledge."

"If you say so," I replied.

My contempt for this man was now so great that I was hardly prepared to grant him any positive qualities.

Layla seemed to guess my thoughts. She smiled for a moment. "Anyway, after a while Capito steered the conversation in question to the dangers of living in the desert. That's what he seemed most interested in. And in the course of that, he began to ask me about the dangerous animals of Africa. As far as I remember, I told him about the predators that were native to Nubia, but then we got to talking about the smaller, but all the more deadly, beasts. I don't remember if he specifically asked me about this topic, or just found it of great interest when I brought it up. But I am sure that I told him about snakes, spiders and scorpions. And other insidious creatures."

She broke off and gave me a meaningful look.

I took a moment, silently expecting her to tell me more—but then I understood what she was getting at with her report.

"The spider in Alma's chamber in Alexandria," I began, seized by sudden excitement. "And the stingers of the scorpions in the fire! Did you also tell the chatterer of this vermin and that custom of your men? That they used to smoke the stingers' poison?"

Layla nodded. "I'm afraid so."

She said nothing more. Her eyes again took on that distant and thoughtful look that I had noticed on her just before.

For a while we sat there in silence, but I could feel that something stood between us. Something unspoken—unspeakable?—that was on Layla's mind.

She might not be my lover anymore, but I told myself I still knew her better than any other man, Marcellus included.

"There's something else that's bothering you," I said when I couldn't stand the silence anymore. "Isn't there? I can see it in your face. Why don't you tell me?"

I grabbed her by the arm, perhaps a bit too roughly, because she pulled away from me. But I achieved what I had intended.

At first she hesitated, and her expression darkened again. But then she seemed to make up her mind.

"It's about Alma," she began, watching me out of the corner of her eye. Her voice had suddenly dropped to a whisper.

"Alma?" I asked, surprised. "What about her?"

Layla once again didn't give me an answer. She really seemed very unwilling to broach the subject, although it was so obviously weighing on her mind.

I reached for her hand, more gently than before, and tenderly sought her gaze.

"Whatever else there is between us, dear," I said, "or there isn't any more—whichever way you look at it—we've always been able to talk to each other freely and honestly. Couldn't we? However delicate a subject it might be."

Layla raised her head. Her eyes met mine. "That's true," she said.

"Good. And that's the way it should stay, I think! And not only because we have another murderer in our midst, whom we shall bring to justice. Won't we? I can't believe that the scribe's death—or the foul spell with the scorpions—were mere misadventures."

Layla nodded. "Neither do I."

"So then—tell me what's on your mind!"

Layla let out a soft sigh, but then she finally spoke up.

"I happened to witness a conversation—between Alma and Lurco," she began, pronouncing the dead barber's name with strange emphasis. "Or rather, I saw the two of them talking to each other. They were too far away for me to understand their words, yet they were arguing.

Fighting, really. There was no mistaking that."

A strange coldness suddenly spread through my stomach—but I wasn't able to offer an explanation as to why.

"Fighting?" I repeated.

Layla nodded, barely noticeably. "In the end, Lurco was so enraged that he raised his voice—very uncharacteristically for him—so I could understand something after all. *Think it over carefully,* he snapped at Alma. *Otherwise you will regret it!* With these words, he strode away."

"Strange," I said. "When was it that you observed this argument?"

"The day after Timotheos died," Layla said.

Her gaze sought mine—but I avoided it. The coldness that I had just felt inside me spread still further. What was Layla getting at with this report?

"I assume you approached Alma about this encounter?" I asked.

"I did."

"And what did she say to that?"

"That Lurco had come to her with a strange lie. He was claiming that he'd seen her at night, how she had gone to that unfortunate meeting with Timotheos. That she left the camp at a late hour and made her way into the desert. Alma insisted that this was a lie. She had the impression that Lurco wanted to ... well, that he wanted to blackmail her or something like that."

"Then, by the words you overheard, he probably meant, *'Think carefully about my offer. If you don't want to pay, you'll regret it.'* That would make sense, wouldn't it?"

"Yes. Probably."

Layla's gaze seemed to literally pierce me.

I shook my head unwillingly. "I wonder how Lurco came to make that strange assertion. Why did he claim to have seen Alma? Just to squeeze money out of her?"

"Lurco was saving up to buy his freedom," Layla replied, "he mentioned that to me once in passing. So he might have been interested in getting a larger sum of money in one fell swoop. And what if he actually saw Alma?" she added in a softer tone.

"What? Nonsense! She said it was a lie, didn't she?"

Layla looked at me wordlessly.

"What do you think?" I asked.

I had raised my voice without having intended it, making my words sound like thunder in my own ears.

"You're not suggesting that *Alma* was lying, are you?" I added, trying hard not to let my inner turmoil show.

Which was hopeless, of course. I knew only too well that I couldn't fool Layla; she had always known how to read me like an open book.

She pulled up her shoulders. "Of course, I don't think Alma is a liar," she said quickly. "But still ... why would Lurco try to blackmail her with an untruth?"

"Do you think if he had spoken the truth, that Alma would then have so readily repeated their conversation to you?" I hissed. My self-control was gone.

"Probably not," Layla said. But she didn't really sound convinced.

"And what do you conclude now from this argument of theirs?" I demanded to know. "Or rather from Lurco's attempt at blackmail? Because that's what it was, wasn't it?"

Layla raised her hands in a dismissive manner. "Nothing, Thanar. I just wanted to let you know. After all, you asked me what was bothering me...."

"Yes, yes. That's all right," I replied.

But the clammy feeling in my stomach would not subside.

XXV

We spent the morning of the next day in our camp, where we gathered in the shade and relaxed for a bit.

Faustinius came out of his tent late; he did not have breakfast, nor did he join us for lunch. Capito seemed unusually taciturn today, and Layla ... she seemed to be avoiding me.

Later in the afternoon we returned to the pyramids, because a very special spectacle had been announced: men from the nearby village of Busiris who were skilled in climbing the almost smooth facade of the great pyramid, were to put on a performance. A breakneck maneuver in which they risked their lives—and a breathtaking spectacle for the audience, as our guide had assured us. A sight that would make the blood boil and that we shouldn't miss at any price.

I did not feel much desire for this spectacle—my blood was already in sufficient turmoil—but Alma was looking forward to the performance with great excitement.

So it happened that she took my arm when it was time to leave the camp and we set off together. We followed Faustinius, who was surrounded by his usual throng of slaves, as well as Capito, who was once again hogging Layla. The midday meal—and several cups of wine—had apparently loosened his tongue, so he was soon up to his usual form. Fortunately, I was not close enough to hear what nonsense he was spouting this time.

We had barely walked a hundred steps when Alma suddenly stopped. She looked back over her shoulder in the direction of the camp.

"I want to grab my cloak quickly," she explained. "Who knows how long we'll be out. And when the sun goes down later, it'll probably cool off again quickly. I'll be right back, okay?"

It was one of the peculiarities of this desert that you thought you'd go up in flames during the day, while at night you would often freeze miserably. The gods of Egypt were not particularly mild towards us humans. Not even to the native people—not to mention strangers like us.

I could have sent one of the lads who formed the closing guard of our small group to retrieve Alma's cloak. But I saw her request as an opportunity to prove my favor to her. So I told her I wanted to see to it myself that she wouldn't feel cold.

Before she could protest, I was already halfway back to the camp. As I said, we hadn't gone very far yet. By the time the group with the women would reach the pyramid, I'd long be with them again. After all, Faustinius was not the kind of eager hiker who'd push for a fast walking pace. It amazed me that he was walking on foot today instead of retiring to his carrying chair and leaving the toil of his transportation to his men.

In Alma's tent I met Zenobia. She had removed the tarp that protected the entrance at night and was cleaning up a bit in the tent.

When she saw me, she was immediately seized with worry. "My mistress?" she asked anxiously.

I raised my hand. "Everything is all right," I said quickly.

"Alma is well. I just came to get her cloak. So she won't be cold, in case we make a late return."

I looked around in the semi-darkness of the tent, but Zenobia immediately rushed to my aid. She opened a clothes chest and took out the neatly folded cloak. With an obliging nod of her head, she handed it to me.

I thanked her and immediately wanted to take my leave.

But she spoke to me, "You'll take good care of my mistress, won't you?" she said. "That no harm comes to her?"

I found the question a little strange. Alma wasn't in any danger, was she?

Since the incident with the spider in Alexandria, nothing had happened that would have amounted to even a dark omen. At least, not as far as Alma was concerned. Unlike Timotheos and Lurco, nothing had happened to *her,* and as far as I could see, she had never been in danger again.

Was Zenobia frightened by the deaths that had befallen our group? Did she see in them—like most others of her rank—the work of dark forces or even angry gods?

Well, she was one of the most fearful and superstitious of the slaves, and she loved her mistress almost idolatrously. One should not be surprised about her worries.

I solemnly promised her that no harm would come to Alma as long as I was by her side.

Zenobia nodded with satisfaction, but then suddenly raised an eyebrow.

"Forgive me for asking, sir," she began, suddenly in a rather cheeky tone, "but I actually thought Layla was your lady of the heart? Now, however, it seems to me that you want to earn Alma's favor?"

"This is really none of your business!" I burst out.

I was certainly not a strict master. I usually dealt with slaves as with freemen, and each of my servants could always address me openly. But what Zenobia took the liberty of doing here ... that clearly went too far! I certainly did not owe her an account of my messed-up love life.

"Forgive me, sir," she said quickly, bowing deeply. "I am merely concerned for my mistress. I wish we could return to our safe home in Rome. We want for nothing there. Now that the master is dead," she added with a frown.

Something about her tone made me listen up and take notice. Instead of finally taking my leave and hurrying back to my friends, I asked Zenobia a question. One that had been on my mind for some time, although I seemed to have only just become aware of it.

"What did he actually die of, your master?" I began. "Was he already old? Or sickly?"

Zenobia seemed surprised by the question. She quickly shook her head.

"No. He died quite suddenly; none of us had expected it. But who can fathom the will of the gods?"

"True enough," I said.

I paused for a moment longer. More questions ran through my mind, but then I decided it was time to go, before Alma started wondering where I had idled for so long.

I quickly left the tent and hurried after my friends.

I had almost caught up with them when I stumbled over a low bush protruding into the path. I almost fell, but I was just able to pull myself up.

Alma's cloak, however, which I had folded neatly over my arm, slipped from me grasp and fell to the ground.

Very annoying. It was an expensive garment made of a gray, finely knitted woolen fabric. The back of the coat and the hem of the hood were decorated with vines— embroidered with magnificent purple thread. A carefully executed handiwork. And Alma seemed to like wearing it very much. She often felt cold and wrapped herself in the cloak almost every evening. And now I had dropped it in the sand!

I quickly bent down, picked it up and shook it out thoroughly. Fortunately, the floor was dry and the garment had apparently not been soiled with dirt.

But just as I was telling myself that, a few spots caught my attention. They were only tiny splashes, at the very bottom hem of the robe and barely visible, being only slightly darker than the fabric itself and of a reddish-brown color.

I carefully felt the hem with my fingers, but it was completely dry. Which didn't surprise me, because as I said, the cloak had slipped away into the sand. Nowhere nearby was there even a drop of water that could have caused the splashes.

The stains had to be older. It was not I who had caused them. That was my conclusion. And they were so small they had probably evaded Zenobia's critical eye and thus escaped cleaning.

Without my being able to stop it, my thoughts took a dark turn: what caused dark splashes and was reddish brown when it dried?

All I could think of was: blood.

XXVI

The sun had already set when we made our way back to camp. The pyramid climbers had proven to be true acrobats and had completely occupied all of our attention.

Even for those of us in the audience, it had been a sweaty spectacle. We had joined the fever and worried whether one of the daring—no, foolhardy!—men would lose their grip on the steep pyramid facade in the next moment and inevitably fall to his death. But everything had turned out smoothly.

When I returned to the camp arm in arm with Alma, I was filled with a wonderful feeling of well-being. I had banished the matter of the cloak from my thoughts. What did a few stains have to mean—even if it really was blood? Surely there was a completely harmless explanation. Alma could have gotten a tiny graze on her leg and perhaps stained the cloak with her own blood. Or something similar.

Above our heads arched a starry sky, showing us the greatness and glory of the gods in the most impressive way.

I heard the cheerful chatter of my companions walking a few steps ahead of us, and I saw how happy and satisfied Alma was. At the spectacle of the pyramid climbers, she had cheered like a young girl and clapped her hands, and even now her eyes were shining.

Once again, she passionately told me how much she was

enjoying our trip. "And your company just as much, Thanar," she added with a shy smile.

My heart leapt, and for a brief moment, all was right with my world.

But no sooner had we reached the camp than I had to turn my attention to more unpleasant things. Optimus came hurrying toward me. His face reflected grimness— coupled with an expression of triumph.

"I caught him," he announced, "and in flagrante too! He had the audacity to sneak into Faustinius' tent. In broad daylight! I followed him stealthily and caught him tampering with the lock of one of the money chests."

My thoughts must have been somewhere else, because I just looked at Optimus uncomprehendingly.

"Capito!" he exclaimed. "I was finally able to expose him as a thief. Just as you suspected. At first he wanted to talk his way out of it, but he was well aware that it wouldn't do him any good. Not with a burglary tool in his hand, kneeling in front of someone else's money chest! I put him under arrest in his tent. I hope that's all right with you, sir? Two of my men are guarding it."

At last I was capable of an appropriate reaction. "Very good work, my Optimus," I praised him. "Has Faustinius been informed yet?"

The next moment it dawned on me that the question was nonsensical. Faustinius had just returned to the camp with me and the others. Optimus could not have had a chance to talk to him yet.

"Sorry, my good man," I said, "I guess I was just a bit—"

I didn't get any further, because at that moment voices were raised at the other end of the camp.

"Oh-ha! He's escaping!" a man's voice shouted.

"Stop him!" roared another. A chorus of wild imprecations erupted.

I whirled around, but Optimus was once again faster than me. By the time I realized what was going on, he had already crossed half of the camp in a flying run.

I followed him as fast as my legs would carry me. Only then did I see what had caused the commotion: Capito had managed to free himself from his tent—which, according to Optimus, had been guarded by two men!

Apparently, the rogue was not only an experienced thief, but also a skilled escape artist. Two skills that probably went hand in hand. Otherwise, he would have long since found himself on a gallows somewhere. Or robbed of his hands, which—depending on the ability of the executioner—could also have led to an imminent death.

With an agility I never thought he had, Capito charged toward that makeshift enclosure at the far end of the camp that housed the draft and riding horses. Usually there were also one or two saddled mounts tied to the fence, as was now the case.

Capito rushed up to one of the horses, had it untied in a single breath, and swung himself onto the animal's back like a fiend. He clicked his tongue and slammed his heels into the flanks of the startled horse, causing it to rear up and gallop away wildly.

One of my guards reached the second horse waiting at the fence before Optimus, swung himself no less nimbly into the saddle and took up the pursuit.

Sand swirled up and robbed us of our vision. Chaos followed. Men cursed, coughed, and rushed on foot after the fleeing scoundrel. Optimus ran at the head of the small squad.

A good four hours passed before I saw the men again.

The night was already far advanced. The camp was illuminated by torches and lamps, the water of the nearby Nile shone silvery in the moonlight, but beyond that all land was plunged into darkness.

Optimus and the other men who had chased Capito returned together. They led the saddled horse, which one of the guards had grabbed, by the reins. The animal was foaming at the mouth, its tongue was hanging out, and its flanks were shining with sweat.

The men looked no less exhausted—and beaten, that could be seen at first glance.

So it was no surprise when Optimus announced to me, shoulders drooping and gasping for breath, "The son of a bitch got away from us. He rode like a demon!"

The men gathered around the servants' fire, quenched their thirst, and washed the desert sand from their eyes and beards in a quickly supplied wooden tub. None of them spoke a word. Their eyes remained fixed on the ground.

Faustinius stepped out of his tent and came hurrying over to me. I put him in the picture about the failure of our men.

When Optimus caught sight of my friend, he jumped up, left his comrades by the fire, and came rushing toward us with his fists clenched.

First he asked Faustinius to forgive him for his shameful

failure, then he raised his head and jutted his chin.

"Will you put some of your horses and your best men at our disposal, sir?" he requested of my friend with a determined look. "Tomorrow at daybreak we can follow our own trail and pursue the criminal further. He has a considerable lead now, but his nag will not carry him forever. We'll get him, I promise you, and then—"

Faustinius raised his hand and silenced him. With a sideways glance at me, he said, "Let the chatterbox go his way for all I care. His chances of crossing the desert alone are hardly worth mentioning. If it is the will of the gods, he will become a meal for the lions this very night. And if not, I don't care either. I will not risk the lives of my best men for this wretch, and Thanar will certainly not want to do without you either. Your place is here in the camp, for the protection of us all."

I could tell Optimus had a retort on the tip of his tongue, but I indicated with a discreet head movement that he should leave well alone.

Before I went back to bed, I went to see Layla in her tent. We had hardly exchanged a word during the day, but now I wanted to discuss Capito's escape with her.

"I don't want to question Faustinius' decision," I said to her. "He was right not to risk the lives of half a dozen good men to capture that scumbag. But in doing so, the murderer of Timotheos and Lurco has also escaped us, I'm afraid. And that doesn't sit well with me at all."

Layla said nothing in reply. Her gaze was heavy and dull, as if she were once again afflicted by a gloomy melancholy.

"My dear?" I asked her, "What do you think about this? Don't you believe it's all coming together nicely? Aren't the deaths at least satisfactorily resolved, if not avenged? Timotheos was spying on our chatterer on behalf of Faustinius. Possibly he had already unmasked him as a thief or, in any case, discovered some evidence against him. For this reason he had to die. Capito lured him out into the desert under a pretext—with the help of a letter from Alma, which he must have forged. Out there he awaited him with drawn blade and attacked him without mercy. That's how it must have been, I think."

Layla tilted her head. "But then why did Timotheos die with Alma's name on his lips?"

"It's obvious," I replied. "He thought she had wanted to meet with him, and then he was stabbed in the back. So he probably didn't even get to see his attacker, and must have assumed that Alma had done him in. As absurd as the very idea may sound."

"And Lurco?" Layla asked in a monotone voice. "He was also killed by Capito?"

"Of course!" I said emphatically.

It upset me to see Layla like this. Brooding, closed, gloomy ... like a woman completely unknown to me.

When she again made no reply, I continued, "I think Lurco witnessed the murder of Timotheos. And because the stupid fellow wanted to get money to buy himself out of slavery, he made a fatal mistake. Instead of betraying the murderer, he tried to blackmail him—and paid for it with his life. Capito devised a diabolical plan to get rid of Lurco, so inconspicuously that it hardly looked like a targeted act of bloodshed. He made use of the scorpion stingers to sow chaos, throwing them into the fire to deprive the men of their senses. They ran out into the night in their madness, and Capito had no difficulty in pursuing Lurco. He lay in wait for him and wounded him with his dagger. Then he relied on the beasts of the desert to do the rest."

Layla eyed me skeptically.

"You said yourself that you told Capito about the poison of the scorpions," I added. "And that the men of your people used to smoke it to obtain visions...."

"That's true," Layla said, but without real conviction.

I looked at her invitingly, but she avoided my glance. Apparently it was impossible to shake her out of her strangely gloomy mood.

Did she perhaps dislike the fact that this murder case had practically solved itself—or rather, had done so thanks to the tireless vigilance of my Optimus? After all, he had confronted Capito and convicted him of being a burglar. The murders had been only an unfortunate consequence of the thieving machinations of our chatterbox. Capito had killed to avoid being exposed as a scoundrel.

In this way, Layla had not had the opportunity to prove her outstanding mental gifts once again. A new triumph as a puzzle solver had eluded her. But I would never have believed that she would take such a thing to heart.

And if she disagreed with me, why was she so silent about it?

XXVII

Over the next few days, we continued our exploration of the pyramids. We attended the rituals held by the Egyptian priests, listened to their lectures on the ancient wisdom of the pharaohs, and mustered the courage to venture inside the great pyramid.

I can't say I was comfortable with the experience. On steep and narrow ramps, we struggled sometimes upward, then downward again, through chambers that were all bare and empty. The air was musty and foul. It seemed to me that it was still the same air that the pharaohs had breathed. Not even as a corpse would I have felt comfortable in this kind of tomb.

I could not forget the masses of stone that surrounded us, seemingly pressing down on us from all sides. My heart was beating in my chest as if it wanted to burst under the weight.

My friend Faustinius, however, could not get enough of the priests' teachings. He was preoccupied with one subject in particular—on which he always asked new questions, no matter what our guides were lecturing about.

"Eternal life," Faustinius began again and again, "can there be a more interesting, a more important subject?"

The bald Egyptian priests seemed to know more about it than any other scholars in the Empire. In fact, they seemed to spend their entire lives studying death, and they also made sure—for a not inconsiderable sum of gold—that the deceased began their journey to the underworld prepared in the best possible way. With their magical characters, the hieroglyphs, they had recorded the knowledge of what trials awaited the soul on the way to immortality, and Faustinius was eager to learn every single word of it.

Was his morbid interest due to the fact that death had been haunting our camp? That two men in the prime of life had already been carried off? Or did Faustinius even fear that his own life was also being sought?

If that was the case, he didn't say a word to me about it. When I once teased him about his so ardent interest in the hereafter, he merely shrugged and said, "We are not younglings anymore, my friend. I'm not, and neither are you. It makes sense to prepare in time ... for the inevitable."

There was no denying that, of course, but I was determined to enjoy all the earthly pleasures on this trip rather than make arrangements for the afterlife.

I bought some art objects for my home from the pushy Egyptian dealers, and I enjoyed my time with Alma.

With each new day I felt I knew her better, appreciated her more ... and what was perhaps the most beautiful thing: to see that she too seemed to connect to me in ever-increasing affection.

For an entire afternoon, Alma and I amused ourselves by deciphering those countless graffiti that lined the base of the pyramid as well as the paws of the mysterious Sphinx.

Finally, we gave a few coins to one of the men who so officiously hawked their services, and he set to work with hammer and chisel to add both our names to those of the uncounted visitors who had already visited this wonder of the world before us.

"Your love for beautiful woman become so immortal," he mumbled with a grin in broken Greek while pointing one of his gnarled fingers at Alma and winking at me. With his other hand, he patted the pyramid's gleaming white stone mantle.

Almost all the teeth were missing from his mouth. His eyesight, however, seemed to still be excellent, just like the dexterity of his withered hands. In no time he had found a free space for our names, and began to hammer nimbly and deftly.

Alma and I looked at each other shyly, and I suddenly felt not only immortal, but also invincible. That was better than poring over the Egyptian Book of the Dead and grilling every available priest about dying, as Faustinius was doing.

In the course of the days, which flowed along like a pleasantly babbling brook, Alma told me about other trips she wanted to take now that she was free, a longing that I could well understand. When she spoke of countries and adventures far away, she seemed even more alive than usual. Her eyes began to shine like the most beautiful gemstones.

I also asked her if she planned to leave Rome and return to her own homeland, the far north. And I spoke to her of Vindobona, that spot of earth that had become home to me and where I felt so comfortable.

"My heart truly doesn't belong to Rome," Alma answered me. "And I would like to get to know it, your Vindobona," she added with a subtle smile. Whereupon, of course, I immediately extended an invitation.

Alma's friendship with Layla, however, took a turn for the worse—for some reason I couldn't figure out. Whereas the two had hit it off right away and had been almost like sisters to each other during the first stops on our tour, it now seemed to me that Layla was avoiding Alma and me.

Was she worried she would be the odd woman out in our company? Did she suddenly feel jealous of my new girlfriend? It had been Layla herself who had wanted to set me up with Alma at all costs!

Yes, my good Ovid, women really were a mystery! It's a fool who might claim otherwise. And an even greater fool, who troubled himself about it!

In truth, everything had turned out for the best, hadn't it? Legate Marcellus would continue to be my good friend, when I finally gave up trying to steal his mistress. And as for Layla and me—we could remain friends, too, after all! We could certainly take further trips ... perhaps in Alma's company, in the future? The two women would become friends again once things were settled between us. At least, that's what I hoped.

For the moment, however, it so happened that the beautiful Northerner and I spent the days together, mostly just the two of us, or in the company of my friend Faustinius. Layla kept aloof, or rather it seemed to me that she sought Zenobia's friendship in a conspicuous way. I observed several times how the two women had long and visibly concentrated conversations with each other.

Once, without intending it, I overheard parts of a conversation between the two. Then I realized that Layla was asking the slave about her mistress. She was doing it in a casual chit-chat tone, as if she were just interested in some gossip, but I knew better. Layla was not a gossipy woman, and if she wanted to get to know Alma better, why not chat with her directly instead of backhandedly pestering the body slave?

I didn't like it, but I decided not to let it spoil the new joy in my life.

I didn't know what was going on inside Layla's head, but if she didn't want to tell me, then I could live with that. I would not pester her. After all, she was no longer my slave and could do as she pleased.

In the meantime, my faithful Optimus kept looking out for Capito. Often I saw him standing somewhere on the edge of the camp at dusk, gazing out into the desert, or restlessly wandering around our tents. He also made sure that my tent, as well as the one in which Faustinius kept his valuables, were always under double guard.

Did he really assume that Capito would dare to return once more and commit another robbery? Or even another murder?

Well, it was better to be safe than sorry, I told myself. And who could really size up this Capito? Obviously not me. I had disliked him from the start, but I had believed him to be nothing more than an annoying show-off. That behind this chatty—yet harmless—facade he was a reckless thief, I would never have dreamed. Or even that he would kill to cover his tracks.

But maybe Optimus was just restless, I told myself. I

could well imagine that a man like him missed the battlefields, the challenge, the danger, the glory, the great deeds ... and maybe even the violence, the bloodshed and the killing?

XXVIII

Finally, we followed the Nile further south and then turned a little to the west, to set up camp on the shore of Lake Moeris.

The next highlight of our tour was the Great Labyrinth. Many scholars also listed it as a wonder of the world in their lists of the greatest showpieces. The famous Pliny was even of the opinion that it eclipsed the pyramids. I was inclined to agree with the man.

Again, as with the other highlights of our tour, we were inevitably taken under the wing of the local guides. But even their erudition, which otherwise seemed so boundless, reached its limits when it came to the Great Labyrinth. None of them could explain to us the original purpose of this enormous complex's construction.

All they could do was make sure we didn't get hopelessly lost in the hundreds, if not thousands, of halls, courtyards, corridors and chambers. Which was no small feat, because the labyrinth didn't bear its name for nothing. Without expert guidance, we would never have found our way around its intricate architecture.

Even if they did not have any solid information, the guides naturally did not refrain from indulging in the wildest speculations about the age, the builder and the possible use of the structure. Some claimed that the labyrinth served the same purpose as the one on Crete: to house a legendary creature like the Minotaur. Others described the labyrinth as the mortuary temple of a pharaoh, as the palace of a demigod, and still others swore that it had been built by priests who had once fled from the legendary island of Atlantis—shortly before it sank beneath the waves.

In any case, it was certain that even Lake Moeris, on the shores of which the labyrinth lay, had largely been created by human hands. Some guides even claimed that the ancient Egyptians had brought it into being entirely artificially.

In the evening, at the campfire, I sat close to Alma for a long time. My limbs were tired, my senses exhausted by the gamut of wondrous impressions.

We talked little, enjoyed the exquisite food that Faustinius's cook prepared for us as he did every evening, and I already fancied myself a favorite of the gods.

The curse of the pharaohs, the misfortune that had seemed to cling to us during the first stops of our tour, had finally left us, of that I was sure. I was convinced that peace had now returned to the camp and that the bloody events of the last few weeks would not be repeated.

I must admit that I was also basking a little in the glow of my skills as a puzzle solver. Obviously I had been right this time, even if Layla didn't want to believe me: Capito was the murderer who had killed Timotheos and Lurco. Since he had fled, we had regained our peace. I wished I could have brought him to justice, but I also just wanted to be content that we had gotten rid of him and that he was no longer bothering us.

When Alma had already gone to sleep, I talked with Faustinius for a while and we drank a few cups of wine together. Layla was also still sitting with us, but she was following our conversation quietly. When Faustinius finally announced that he wanted to go to sleep, she and I were left alone.

The fire had already burned down to embers, the night was cold—and the mood between us was just as frosty. I would have liked to talk to her about what had come between us, but I couldn't find the right words.

Instead, I emptied my cup, offered to walk her to her tent, and then designed to go to bed as well.

Silently, I walked beside her. The silence of the night enveloped us, and my heart grew heavy.

Before disappearing into her tent, she pressed a shy kiss to my cheek.

I paused for a moment, hesitating about what to do, but finally I turned and left. My head was full of questions, but I was tired and longed for my soft bed.

Only a few torches were still burning at the edge of the camp. I saw Optimus and the other guards who had taken up their positions for the night. Dark clouds were gathering in the sky. Perhaps there would be rain? A truly rare spectacle in Egypt.

In the semi-darkness I entered my tent and prepared to undress. I threw my belt and tunic over a chest and walked blindly the few steps in the direction where I knew my bed to be.

I bent down to lift the blanket and sink down onto the mattress—then I froze, startled by an angry hiss.

I could barely make anything out, but the blanket whose

corner I had managed to grab suddenly seemed to be moving on its own under my hand.

Startled, I let go of it. What was this hideous haunting?

XXIX

Again there was a hissing noise—and suddenly I knew what that sound was: the angry utterings of a snake!

I sent a fast prayer to the gods and backed away. My limbs hardly wanted to move. I knew that any jerky gesture could mean my end.

How well are snakes able to see in the dark? The question popped into my head. But I didn't want to linger to find out.

Step by step I retreated—then I turned and ran. I fled from the tent and shouted for a guard with a torch or lamp. "Over here! To me!" I shouted.

A fellow with a lantern rushed to my aid. Optimus appeared immediately after him.

"What's the matter with you, sir?" he cried, startled.

With a jerk, he looked around, his gaze hurrying over the boundaries of our camp. With tightened shoulders he prepared himself for an attack.

"Your sword," I commanded him.

He handed it to me without hesitation.

I turned and walked the few steps back to my tent, determined now, though still filled with fear.

Optimus and the lamp bearer followed on my heels.

I lifted the tarp that revealed the entrance to the tent and looked around in the dim glow of the lamp.

The blood froze in my veins. A monstrous reptile was writhing on my bed. The body was half hidden under the blanket, but the head curved upright above the neck.

It was a snake, definitely not one native to the northern lands. It had to be a good six or seven feet long. Its skin was blackish brown, the belly a little lighter. The head was enormous, wedge-shaped, but the most imposing thing was the neck shield, which the beast now spread furiously. It looked like the bust of a pharaoh.

"Let me kill it," I heard Optimus urging behind me.

He pushed to my side, wanted to snatch the sword from me and rush toward the reptile, but I was faster. I lunged, swung the blade and slashed with all my might.

An angry hiss could still be heard—then the reptile's head fell from its neck. The fire in the demonic eyes went out.

My knees buckled under me. Suddenly I felt as if I had eaten spoiled food, my guts rebelling at the sight of the decapitated reptile. But I held myself steadfastly upright and left the tent with a brisk step.

I must have yelled so loudly for a torchbearer earlier that half the servants were on their feet by now. I had roused them from their sleep, and apparently Layla, too, who now came rushing toward me from her tent clad only in a thin white robe.

On the other side of the camp, I caught sight of Zenobia, who was also hurrying toward me. But of Alma, her mistress, there was no sign.

Optimus did not leave my side. "I can't imagine that such a beast would have found its way into your tent all by itself," he whispered in my ear.

He was undoubtedly right about that. I found it just as difficult to imagine as he did.

"What happened, master?" cried Layla. Once again she fell back into the old form of address. Her eyes were wide with terror.

I pointed to my tent. "A snake ... has crept in," I said.

"*Crept in?*" she repeated.

She raised her eyebrows and hurried toward my tent. If she had been Alma, I would have held her back to spare her the sight of the monstrous decapitated reptile. But with Layla such a concern was unfounded.

She disappeared into the tent—and a moment later actually came back to me with the severed head of the snake on her palm. I really had not expected that.

She twisted and turned the disgusting trophy with her fingers as if she were merely studying the anatomy of a beautiful flower. In the process, she stained her hands all over with the dark red blood of the snake.

"Put that down!" I cried, turning my head away in disgust.

Layla did me the favor. She carefully got down on her knees and put the snake's head in the sand. I couldn't help feeling that this was not the first time she had encountered such a reptile.

"Another one of those desert animals that look like the spawn of hell, yet are harmless?" I asked her.

I forced myself to smile, even though I didn't feel like it one bit. Nevertheless, after the encounter with the tarantula in Alma's room, I hoped that Layla would give me the all-clear.

She, however, remained serious and shook her head.

"This is pretty much the most dangerous snake far and wide," she explained to me. "The uraeus snake. It is familiar to me from my homeland, and even for an adult person its venom is absolutely deadly. As far as I have heard it here from the natives, Cleopatra is said to have taken her own life with the help of such a snake. A quick, merciful death. And the corpse is hardly disfigured in the process, which must have been very important to the beautiful pharaoh."

What a nice little detail on the side ... Layla almost sounded like one of our learned tour guides. I was at a loss for words.

"This reptile does not fear the proximity of humans," she continued. "It occasionally sneaks into villages, looking for a warm place to spend the night or some food in the pantries."

"Then you think this beast found its way into my tent all by itself?" I said.

A weight lifted from my chest. Was it just an unfortunate coincidence that I had escaped by a hair's breadth? Not an attempt on my life?

I couldn't have said whether I could still believe this at that point, after everything that had already happened to us in the last weeks and months. But I definitely wanted to believe it!

Optimus interfered. "I'm telling you, it was Capito!" he cried with fervor. "He has returned and now wants to take his revenge! He must have sneaked into the camp during the day, when most of us were visiting the labyrinth."

"His revenge?" I repeated. "On me? Why would he want to do that?" The chatterbox had neither tried to steal from me—at least, as far as I knew—nor had I personally pursued or threatened him.

Capito had become a fixed idea for Optimus by now, it seemed to me. The glorious veteran probably could not cope with the fact that the villain had escaped him.

I wanted to talk some sense into Optimus, but just at that moment, out of the corner of my eye, I noticed a movement near me.

I turned my head—and saw that Zenobia had made something disappear into the pockets of her robe. Something she had just picked up from the floor.

"What have you got there?" I inquired of her.

"Nothing, sir," she replied quickly, moving to hurry away.

I, however, followed behind her. My mood was—as one can probably imagine—at a low point. I could not bear any more secrets.

I caught up with the slave and grabbed her, perhaps a touch too roughly, by the arm.

A strangled cry escaped her.

"I want to see what you picked up!" I demanded. "Right now!"

She looked at me, frightened. As if paralyzed, her hand went into her pocket and brought out a sparkling jewel. Zenobia narrowed her eyes and held it out to me with an outstretched hand.

It was a golden fibula, dust-covered, yet shining. At its end sat a sparkling turquoise gemstone.

I dropped the jewel back into Zenobia's hand as if it were red-hot iron. I knew this fibula. Alma used it to close her cloak when she was shivering.

Zenobia had found the piece of jewelry in the immediate vicinity of my tent—where Alma had not been all day. At least not as far as I knew. She must have come secretly, but for what purpose?

I refused to believe that my new lady of the heart could have anything to do with the vile reptile in my tent.

XXX

The rest of the night I tossed and turned sleeplessly on my bed. I struggled with myself, trying to decide whether I should confront Alma about the fibula, and I wondered who could want to kill me, of all people.

What connected me to Timotheos and Lurco, who had also been attacked, and had not made such a lucky escape as I had? Had I been completely wrong with regard to the pretty theory I had formed about Capito as the culprit of the bloody deeds?

Or did I see crime where there was none? Had the snake not been brought into my tent by human hands? Had we, in the end, angered the gods of Egypt, as so many of our slaves believed?

Far too many questions—and not a single useful answer to show for it. I no longer knew what to believe.

When the sun had risen, I waited until it was civil to pay Alma a visit. Then, however, I hurried to her tent. I wanted—I needed—an explanation from her.

She seemed pleased to see me, although a little surprised at the early hour.

I would have loved to tell her how beautiful she looked. Her eyes were still narrow from sleep, her hair not yet pinned up into one of the complicated hairstyles she loved to wear.

But I had not come to flatter her.

"Were you happy to get your fibula back?" I began without mincing words. "A very valuable piece, isn't it? How terrible if it had been lost to you."

She raised her eyebrows. "My fibula? Zenobia brought it to me in the night. I have no idea how it could have been lost...."

"What amazes me is *where* you lost it," I said.

She looked at me uncomprehendingly.

"Very close to my tent, Alma. And you must have lost it yesterday during the day, because I remember seeing it on your cloak the night before last."

"I always wear it on my cloak," Alma replied, "to close it when I'm cold. But yesterday I was nowhere near your tent, Thanar."

"That's what I assumed, actually," I said. The words came out of my mouth harshly. I did not manage to keep my displeasure completely to myself.

"*Assumed*?" Alma repeated.

Her warm, green-brown eyes, which I liked so much, widened. "What are you talking about?" she asked. "You know we weren't in camp all day yesterday. You picked me up here in the morning ... and when we returned from the labyrinth, you accompanied me all the way to my tent. In the evening we dined together by the fire, but that's not anywhere near your tent. So I can't have lost the fibula where you claim."

She eyed me with a questioning look. "But why does it even matter where the thing was? Do you think someone stole it—and then lost it from their possession?"

She interrupted herself abruptly. A new thought seemed

to have just occurred to her. One that visibly put her in turmoil. "Are you afraid Capito may have returned—to steal from us again?" she asked, her voice suddenly quivering. "Or worse?"

I remained silent. I didn't want to say the words that were on the tip of my tongue. The idea that they could be true was just too terrible.

The look on my face must have told Alma everything. "W-wait," she stammered, "you're not thinking about Capito at all, are you? You believe that I...."

She faltered. Her voice had broken with the last words.

She looked at me in silence for a while, obviously trying to collect herself. Then she continued, barely audibly: "Zenobia told me this morning about the deadly snake in your tent. Possibly another sign from the gods, she thought in her superstition. Or the attack of a mortal? This time on you, Thanar?"

"It looks like it, yes," I replied curtly.

She backed away from me. "And you think I brought that vile reptile into your tent?"

"Did you?" I asked. The words had an aftertaste like bitter bile. Nevertheless, I forced myself to say them.

I cannot describe the expression that came over Alma's face.

"You seriously think I could want to ... kill you?" she whispered, barely audible. "Don't you understand anything? I would have thought that in the last days and weeks I have made it very clear to you what I—"

She did not complete the sentence, leaving the words and all the painful emotion associated with them standing between us. A wall as high and wide as the one in Babylon.

She averted her eyes from me. "I think you should go, Thanar," she said.

I left with a heavy heart.

As if even the desert wanted to mock me in my confusion, shortly thereafter the sky darkened, and around noon a sandstorm swept over our camp.

Our slaves and guards did a great job. All our tents and wagons, the draft and riding animals, the supplies, everything was well fastened and remained intact. Although it would later take hours to clean it all again, of the thick layer of sand that had settled into every crack, onto every surface.

I spent the day in the large living tent of Faustinius and immersed myself in reading. However, I was hardly in the mood for more love wisdom from the pen of Ovid. So I read an enjoyable novel called *Satyricon*. Or rather, I attempted to.

No matter how hard I tried, the words would not enter my head. They remained pale and meaningless, and my thoughts wandered here and there.

"Are you brooding over a difficult decision, my old friend?" Faustinius finally addressed me.

The scroll slipped from my hands.

"What?" I asked, irritated and in rather rude fashion.

Faustinius smiled mildly. "Do you think I don't see what is bothering you, friend?"

Was it really that obvious?

Probably because I didn't answer him, Faustinius continued: "It's no use, this dark brooding and dithering!

Listen to me! Only the man who dares can also win. You must show courage, Thanar."

"Dare? Win? Courage?" I repeated dully.

Faustinius laughed, came over to me and slapped me on the shoulder. "What's the matter with you? I've never seen you like this. Be stout-hearted, my friend, and leave the past behind you!"

I had not the slightest idea what he was talking about. His words did not fit in any way with the subject that was actually occupying me.

"Alma!" he exclaimed, after I had once again failed to answer him. "You should propose to her! What are you waiting for? I can see how you feel about her, and she for you, my friend. You've finally realized that by now, haven't you?"

He sat down with me on the bench and waved a slave over to serve us refreshments.

"Layla feels a lot for you," Faustinius continued, "but it is friendship, not passion. Not the love you long for. That probably belongs to your friend, the legate. Alma, on the other hand ... she could be yours. Oh, what am I talking about, she already is! She is ready for your proposal!"

I nodded silently.

How could I make my old friend understand that my thoughts were in completely different realms right now? Anywhere but marriage.

XXXI

When I stepped out of my tent the next morning, a bright blue sky greeted me. Our servants had scrubbed and cleared the entire camp of dust, so that one might have thought the sandstorm of the previous day had merely been a bad dream.

I had agreed with Faustinius that we would go on a very special excursion today. On the other shore of Lake Moeris was a place of worship called Crocodilopolis, the sanctuary of the crocodile god, as one could easily gather from the name.

Layla had already announced that she wanted to join us on this excursion, and I myself had assigned Optimus to accompany us. Not because I was anxious and wanted to call on the protection of my faithful veteran, but to take his mind off things. Capito's escape still seemed to weigh on his thoughts, and I calculated that the spectacle that awaited us at the Crocodile Sanctuary might at least distract him somewhat. He was in desperate need of cheering up—just as I was myself.

Faustinius devoted himself to a sumptuous meal full of sweets shortly before our planned departure, while I made up my mind.

I could not bear how I had taken my leave of Alma the day before. Or rather how she had expelled me, visibly offended, from her tent.

So I went to her to invite her to join our tour to

Crocodilopolis as well.

When I called her name in front of her tent, I received no answer at first. I looked around for Zenobia, whom I could send with a message into the tent of her mistress. Simply entering Alma's space without being asked was out of the question for me.

The faithful slave, who usually hung around near her mistress all the time, did not appear however. Even after I had called loudly for her a few times and asked some passing slaves about her whereabouts.

But finally, Alma herself lifted the tarp that closed the entrance to her tent. She stuck her head out and looked at me. I thought I could read in her features a mixture of reservation, yet also joy at seeing me.

I did not apologize for what I had implied the day before. Instead, I directly extended my invitation to her to accompany us to Crocodilopolis.

Her features brightened.

"I'd love to," she said, "I just want to finish dressing quickly."

She lowered the tarp and disappeared inside the tent.

"Where is your slave this morning?" I called after her. Never before had I seen Alma get dressed without Zenobia's help.

I did not receive an answer.

When Alma finally left the tent with a less than perfect hairstyle and came toward me, I repeated my question. "What about Zenobia?"

It was as if I had asked for rope in the house of a hanged man. Alma's brow furrowed.

"I set her free," she said somberly. "And sent her away,

early this morning. She will probably be on her way back to Alexandria by now. I gave her money and everything she will need to stand on her own two feet from now on," she added quickly.

"But that's ... very generous of you," I replied haltingly. "Forgive me for saying so, but this comes quite unexpected for me."

Alma eyed me with a touch of defiance. She clearly had no desire to justify herself to me.

"Well, it may be unexpected for you," she said, "but it's not for me. I had been tired of her for some time. I should have sent her away much earlier, if only I'd had the heart to do so. Her never-ending care and maternal attitude suffocated me. The way she followed my every move, whether I wanted her to or not ... almost like my late husband!"

Alma shook her head vigorously. A golden strand of hair came loose from her hairdo and fell into her face.

I resisted the impulse to push it back behind her ear with a tender gesture.

"I couldn't stand it any longer," she continued in an angry tone. "Zenobia's anxiety and constant desire to return home at last ... it almost spoiled this journey for me. I've been longing for this trip for half my life!"

She raised her eyes and looked at me challengingly. "I want to be free at last, Thanar. Never again shall anyone tell me what to do or what not to do! Be it out of even the most well-intentioned concern for my well-being."

Suddenly and almost silently, Layla appeared next to me. She gave Alma a strange look and greeted us both only with a nod of her head. Had she overheard our conversation?

"We are ready to go," she said, gesturing with her hand over her own shoulder.

I turned around and saw that Faustinius had already made himself comfortable in his carrying chair, and a good dozen slaves surrounded him. Optimus was also standing with the group. His gaze wandered around in restless vigilance as always, but his posture seemed somewhat relaxed. That was a start, after all.

I offered Alma my arm, and after a brief, barely noticeable hesitation, she took it. We joined our friends on foot. We had to walk only a few hundred steps to the landing place at the lake, where a spacious boat was already waiting for us. Crocodilopolis lay on the far shore of the lake.

The cult site of the sacred crocodile was very popular with tourists, we had been told—and it fully lived up to the reports we had heard and read about it.

When we arrived at the sanctuary and could admire the first monumental statues of the crocodile god, I had to think back to how Capito had described these monstrous beasts of the Nile to us shortly after our arrival in Egypt. And I also remembered those physical specimens that we had later been able to observe with our own eyes on the river.

For once, Capito's words had not been an exaggeration. Neither with regard to the enormous dimensions of the animals' bodies—we had been able to observe specimens a good twenty-five feet long when we had sailed upstream on the Nile—nor when it came to their teeth and jaws. They were almost more hideous than the chatterer had described them to us. The crocodiles could easily kill an adult human being, or even a fully-grown cow.

Our Nile barque, the same one that Faustinius had hired, was a spacious and very robust ship, so we hadn't feared for our lives. But the very idea that one of these armored beasts could ram us had made us feel quite queasy.

Of course, crocodiles—like so many other animals in this land of sorcerers and necromancers—were also worshiped as gods. And just as one could admire the holy Apis Bull in the flesh in Memphis, one encountered the living crocodile god in the sanctuary of Crocodilopolis.

From a safe distance, we were able to observe how the priests first fed the sacred animal with the offerings we had brought along—and then in defiance of death, cleaned its teeth! These men were true believers. They placed their lives in the hands—or rather in the mighty jaws—of their god.

It was like staring into the throat of a lion in the arena of an amphitheater. No, worse, because the crocodile's jaws were incomparably larger, and armed with even more fearsome teeth than those of any lion.

Crocodilopolis and the feeding spectacle I've just described were so popular with travelers that the blessed crocodile had become morbidly obese. On its already short legs it could only waddle along lazily. One may forgive me this observation; of course, I don't want to appear disrespectful to any deity!

When we returned to the camp that evening, tired and dusty, the feeling of happiness that I had felt before the incident with the uraeus snake had returned to me. I had almost forgotten the attempt on my life—if it had actually been one.

Reckless of me? Foolish even?

Probably.

When the sun was already disappearing behind the horizon, I set out once again to stretch my legs on the lakeshore. The evening air was still warm, but the heat of the day was already over. I felt light and carefree.

But I was not allowed to enjoy this cozy atmosphere for long.

XXXII

I had barely taken a few steps away from the camp when Layla appeared at my side.

Once again, I had not heard her coming, my black Sphinx. But that did not surprise me anymore. I was pleased to find that the sight of her, and the familiar sound of her voice, accelerated my heart beat only slightly. The days when I had been pining half-madly for her seemed to be finally over now.

I had truly not expected this when I had set out on this journey with Layla, but the gods obviously had other plans for me. For which I was grateful to them.

Layla, however, did not seek my company out of romantic motives. Her forehead was deeply wrinkled, her gaze gloomy.

"We need to talk, Thanar," she said in a tone that would not have been unexpected at a funeral. On such a balmy, carefree late summer evening, it seemed completely out of place.

"What grieves you, dear?" I said lightly.

I half expected—or still hoped, after all?—that she would confess her jealousy to me. That now that I was ready to give my heart to another, she had finally realized what I meant to her. What she would lose if she didn't fight for me.

But far from it!

"I wish I were wrong," she said in a serious voice. "Just

this once. But I fear I can no longer close my eyes to the truth, as much as it pains me. Not when I think your life is in danger, Thanar."

My romantic reveries came to an abrupt end. My life ... in danger?

"Now that Zenobia has supposedly been set free," she continued, "my worst fears have been realized. Yes, I suppose that's how it is. I'm sorry, Thanar."

"*Supposedly* been set free? What on earth are you talking about?" I asked, suddenly indignant.

Did I already suspect what terrible accusation Layla was about to pronounce? Had I just closed my own eyes to the bitter truth all this time, even though it was staring me in the face so conspicuously?

"Alma," she whispered, "I fear—oh, I don't know how to put it!—that her spirit is clouded? Her soul is filled with darkness? An evil demon may have made her commit the terrible deeds, but what difference does it make?"

She interrupted herself and looked at me sorrowfully. I could see how difficult these words were for her. But she did not let herself be distracted.

She cleared her throat, then said in a firm voice, "Alma is the one who has brought misfortune and death upon us. I am so sorry. She is the murderer of Timotheos. And of Lurco. And almost of you, too. I fear she will not rest until this last, worst act of blood is done."

I stood there as if struck by lightning.

"You must be mistaken," I protested.

But I spoke without real conviction. My words sounded hollow in my own ears.

I had to think back to Alma's fibula, which had been lost

so close to my tent, and at a time when she claimed to have come nowhere near the place.

"I truly wish I were wrong," Layla repeated, "I was very fond of Alma. No, more than that. I even thought I had found a true friend in her. And I hoped she could give you what I..."

She broke off, lowering her gaze. "Well, what I can't give you, Thanar. At least, not in the way you want it. And in the way you deserve!"

She nodded vigorously, probably to reinforce her words. At the same time, she looked at me as if she wanted to ask for my forgiveness.

Now it was my turn to avert my gaze. I could not bear that pleading expression on her face. But even less could I bear her words.

However, she continued mercilessly: "I made the mistake of letting myself be blinded by my feelings. That's the only reason I didn't want to see what has been obvious for so long. Alma killed her own husband, Thanar. That's where it started. I coaxed the story out of Zenobia—without her realizing it. She would never have betrayed her mistress, but what she told me was proof enough. In the house of Alma's husband, who was a medicus, the right herbs could be found to send a man to the afterlife. And Alma knows her way around them; I have convinced myself of that. Her husband was a monster who tortured and mistreated her, so she had every reason to wish him dead. But I think she didn't stop at wishing. She helped herself."

"Nonsense," I exclaimed. "How can you be sure of that? The man is dead, buried, and we didn't even know him.

Only the gods can say what he may really have died of."

Layla nodded. "If you say so. But we did know Timotheos. And we also knew he was courting Alma. That he wanted to win her as his wife, didn't he? And that he died after a letter from her lured him out of camp at night. He even died with her name on his lips, have you forgotten that? With his last breath he accused her. But we did not want to hear it."

I shook my head, inflamed with sudden anger. "You say she killed him merely because he ... was courting her? Are you out of your mind?"

Layla closed her eyes.

When she opened them again, her voice sounded downright tortured. "I told you that she must be afflicted with a dark delusion. Her husband may have tormented her so much that she now hates all men. That she wants to take revenge on them—on all of them, even those who have done her no harm at all. Like Timotheos. Or you, Thanar."

"This is completely insane!" I exclaimed.

"It is. But still, it is true. There is no other explanation, no better motive that can be found. But the facts can't be challenged. Don't you see that, master?"

"And Lurco?" I cried heatedly. "He certainly wasn't interested in winning Alma's favor!"

"That is true. I think he had to die because his greed was his undoing, we've already discussed that. He must have witnessed the first act—Timotheos's murder. Or maybe he just suspected something, saw the scribe going into the desert at night ... and that Alma had followed him. I suppose Lurco tried to blackmail her. He was saving up to buy his freedom, and the sum he hoped to collect would surely have come in handy. He was a witness who had to be silenced forever."

I felt as if I were about to lose my mind myself. Like the dark demons Layla spoke of, her words forced themselves on me, drilled into my head, stabbed and cut into my innermost being.

"I can't imagine how Alma would know about the poison of those scorpions," I protested. "With whose stings the men at the fire were driven mad and Lurco rendered defenseless."

I looked at her challengingly. I was far from ready to believe what Layla was claiming.

But my resistance was born of desperation. I knew all too well the almost unerring instinct of my former slave. I myself had already witnessed twice how Layla had unmasked criminals and hunted them down.

And that the third should now be Alma, *my* Alma, as I'd come to call her in the meantime. Secretly, of course, but still....

"Just think, master," cried Layla, looking as if she shared every pain I felt. "Alma's body slave is a Nubian like myself. And I am well acquainted with the vermin that dwell in Egypt. Why should it be any different with Zenobia? Her mistress will have elicited this knowledge from her. Certainly in an unobtrusive way—but it was all she needed for her plans."

I objected again, "But the tarantula ... it was supposed to attack Alma herself, wasn't it? After all, the vermin was smuggled into her chamber! And then the incident in Rhodos. Where Alma was almost killed by a roof tile. She can't be the murderer we're looking for, Layla! After all, she almost became a victim herself."

The look Layla gave me was the kind usually given to defiant children. *You know better,* her eyes seemed to tell me. *As much as you may protest.*

Yet she continued to speak patiently, seeming willing to play along with my desperate attempts at denial.

"The tarantula is a harmless creature," she said, "we've discussed that too. It certainly looks scary, and an ignorant person might think it deadly. But an insider does not. I think Alma brought it into her room to divert any subsequent suspicion from herself. To make us believe that she was an innocent victim—while secretly she may have already conceived the plan to murder Timotheos. And the roof tile may have been a real accident," Layla added. "A bad omen perhaps, a warning from the gods that we just didn't know how to interpret properly. I told you I saw a dark shadow, back in Rhodos, when the tile fell from the roof. Do you remember? A shadow behind which I suspected an assassin ... but I may have been mistaken. Maybe it really was just a stray animal that set the tile loose."

"We can all be mistaken," I replied, "but what if you're wrong now, too? When it comes to Alma's guilt...."

"I wish with all my heart that it were so," she replied. "For your sake, Thanar. I thought she could be the woman for you that I would love to be, if there were not another man dwelling in my heart."

"You already said that," I mumbled glumly.

A hard lump sat in my throat. How I would have liked to hold Layla in my arms right now. And Alma! Her even more than my former lover. I was only really realizing that now.

What a cruel irony of fate. I had finally succeeded in giving my heart to a woman who seemed to return my feelings—and now she was supposed to be a murderess?

I swallowed hard and tried to cling to the last objections that haunted my mind. "Putting that spider into her bed herself ... that's not the act of a madwoman, is it?" I pleaded. "To plan ahead so carefully as to clear yourself of any subsequent suspicion?"

Layla frowned, but she was a merciless judge. She swept away even this objection like a withered leaf in the desert wind.

"We cannot see into the human heart, Thanar. Especially not when it is under the spell of a dark demon. On the outside, a human may seem perfectly normal, harmless even. But inside, a deadly fire may burn."

I didn't know what else to say.

Layla, on the other hand, took the floor again. "I don't think Zenobia has gained her freedom. I think she's long dead and buried under a nearby sand dune."

She looked around as if she could track down the corpse with the naked eye. "Surely Zenobia had put it all together before now. She loved her mistress, I have no doubt, but not enough to keep silent forever about her actions. She was a danger to Alma. That's why she had to die—just like Lurco."

For a long while Layla and I stood on the shore of the lake. The last light of the day shone on the mirror-smooth surface. Waterfowl chattered in the reeds.

"What do you want to do now?" I finally said to Layla.

"What has to be done, master. We have to confront Alma and make her confess. And after that..."

I raised my hand, silencing her. I could not bear to hear what she was undoubtedly going to say. It tore my heart in two to think about the punishment that would await Alma. A cruel death that I could never wish upon her, even if I now had to realize that she herself had wanted to take my life.

Was the beautiful and gentle Alma in truth like the beast that she had put into my bed? A deadly snake, which I the lonely fool had nourished at my breast?

"Let me think about it," I said to Layla, "Then I will confront Alma myself."

But no sooner had I spoken the words than I knew that I didn't want to leave it at just thinking. I needed certainty. Absolute certainty.

I turned back to Layla, "I want to put your words to the test. You say that Alma kills because men worship her, get too close to her, don't you?"

Layla looked at me questioningly. "Yes?" she said cautiously.

"Well, that can be checked, can't it? I will provoke another attack by courting Alma all the more passionately now. If you are right in your accusation, this will push her to a new attack on my life. And this time I want to catch her in the act! Then we will have irrefutable proof of her guilt."

Layla's eyes widened in fright. Then she shook her head violently.

"You'd be risking your life on this plan," she cried. "I won't let you!"

"What is my life to you?" I retorted. "Your heart belongs to Marcellus, you already said that."

She opened her mouth, but immediately closed it again. Something sparkled in her dark eyes that I didn't know how to name. But in the end she did not contradict me.

"You see, that's answer enough for me," I said bitterly.

Whereupon she found her tongue again. "Oh, Thanar. It's not that simple."

I turned away and made my way back to camp.

XXXIII

Instead of directing my steps to Alma's tent that same evening, I returned to my own. I had a lamp brought to me before I entered it, making sure that no new and deadly surprise awaited me.

I'm happy to report that no new vermin was to be found in my bed. Gripped by gallows humor, a bitter laugh escaped me.

I tossed and turned sleeplessly on my bed until the early morning. I went over each of Layla's arguments in my mind—but no matter how hard I tried, I could find no fault in her accusations.

When the new day dawned, I set about putting the plan I'd come up with into action. I would not deviate from it, even if it should mean my end! I would woo Alma more intensively than I had done so far. And if she really were a maniacal man-killer, she would inevitably seek my life with renewed fervor.

What's next, I thought grimly.

In what hideous way would Alma try to finish me off—if Layla really were right?

It seemed to me that we had already exhausted the poisonous animals of Egypt—which, of course, did not mean that one couldn't murder in a hundred more very similar ways.

Playing the bait in this way—by wooing Alma—was easy for me. My affection for her was unbroken in spite of everything, and she also seemed to feel nothing but joy at the fact that I now spoke quite openly about my feelings for her. Yes, I even went so far as to suggest that she move to Vindobona. She herself had told me that she detested life in Rome. So why not travel north and perhaps make a home in a charming little provincial town?

I discussed with Faustinius that I wanted to stay a few more days in our current camp. I didn't have to elaborate what kind of sightseeing activities I was still planning here—he simply nodded and agreed with my suggestion. After that we should go back to Alexandria via the Nile, back across the Mare Nostrum and further to the last station of our world wonder-route. To Olympia, to see the imposing statue of Zeus by Phidias.

So during the day I courted Alma, but at night I lay sleepless in my tent, clutching my short sword. I had to be prepared when the expected attack finally came.

All the while, I ate and drank nothing that was not served to our entire group, and at every step I took, I always glanced over my shoulder with a watchful eye. I expected Alma to suggest a romantic tryst far from camp, and each evening when I returned to my tent, I first subjected it to a closer inspection.

But Alma neither did anything during the day that seemed suspicious to me, nor did my night watches bring any results. On the contrary, those days became the most beautiful and carefree I had spent in a long time. Well, maybe not entirely carefree, because the knowledge that Layla was probably right hung over me like the sword of

Damocles.

I ordered Optimus to stay away from my tent at night. After all, I wanted to give the alleged murderess the opportunity to sneak into my tent with a pointed dagger or some other insidious weapon.

Optimus, of course, protested vehemently at first, but as a legionary he was also used to obeying orders, and so he finally complied with my instructions.

At least that's what I thought.

The first night I way lying in wait, I heard footsteps near my tent, and as I crept quietly to the exit and peered out into the darkness, I recognized a shadow.

It was not Alma. Nor was it an assassin she had hired. It was Optimus, whom I angrily confronted.

He was contrite and assured me that he would not sleep if he knew me unguarded. It was difficult for me to reprimand him harshly and banish him to the servants' area. But what choice did I have if I wanted to go through with my plan?

In the following nights I did not see him again.

My regular night watch, however, took its toll. It became more and more difficult for me not to sink into sleep, and during the day I was increasingly overcome by fatigue, which didn't exactly help my courtship of Alma.

Sometimes I would steal away for a few hours, telling Alma that Faustinius wanted to see me—only to catch up on some much-needed rest in his tent.

It was the fourth of these nights when I finally slipped into a strange waking sleep. My eyelids were open, but dream images began to rise in my mind's eye. Was this what happened when you denied yourself sleep for too long? Did you begin to lose your mind? Or were these images messages from a deity? From a demon?

In rapid succession, all the events of the past weeks came back to me. The bad omens, the minor accidents and finally the bloody deeds—I saw them all pass me by again like dark dream images. They were distorted, grotesque, terrifying, but I could not suppress them.

Then suddenly something Layla had said to me during that accusation she'd made against Alma came to my mind.

Zenobia is a Nubian like myself. I am very familiar with the vermin that dwell in this land. Why should Zenobia be any different? Her mistress will have elicited this knowledge from her, inconspicuously certainly....

It was as if each of these words had burned itself into my memory. But now, completely without my doing, they suddenly took on a whole new meaning. It was as if a bright flash of lightning exploded in my head. A divine finger pointing, which finally led me to the correct realization!

Alma's slave—she was the key! Zenobia, who knew about the deadly animals of the land. Zenobia, who had found Alma's fibula near my tent. Zenobia, who saw dark omens everywhere, and who seemed far more devoted to her mistress than any other slave I knew. Yes, she cared so much for Alma that the latter had finally sent her away because she'd felt deprived of her freedom.

The images blurred, no matter how hard I tried to hold on to them. I knew they were trying to tell me something important—but another sensation suddenly began to displace them. A pungent smell crept into my nose. What kind of a strange dream was this now?

My eyes were still open. I even went so far as to feel my eyelids with my fingers to make sure. I was not asleep.

The smell became stronger. Voices were raised at the edge of my consciousness. Excited voices. Then I heard footsteps.

Is this the end? went through my mind. Had the murderers Alma had hired come to finish me off?

The acrid stench crept into my throat and made me cough.

Panting, I pulled myself up from my bed. Outside, the entire camp seemed to have come to life. A whole army of torchbearers? Because suddenly it was bright around me, although also foggy at the same time.

XXXIV

I shook my head, rubbing my temples. I finally had to wake up, I needed all my senses to be active!

And then I understood. There was no army of torchbearers out there, but a fire! In our camp! And the fog that threatened to envelop me was smoke.

The next moment there was a crackling behind me. As I whirled around, now finally halfway stable on my feet, my tent was already on fire.

This finally snapped me out of my lethargy.

I seized my blade, grabbed the blanket from my bed and gathered it up. Then I wrapped it around my head and shoulders, ducked and rushed toward the exit.

The searing heat of the flames washed over me. I held my breath, ignored the burning in my chest, and courageously jumped out into the open. I rolled a few feet across the ground, then quickly inspected and felt my robes. Fortunately for me, they weren't on fire.

I struggled to my feet.

All the servants seemed to be up and scurrying around. People came rushing out of their tents screaming, men armed with buckets were running towards the lake.

I recognized Layla, who was hurrying across the camp—not in my direction, but toward Alma's tent. Did she want to rush to her aid?

No, I realized bitterly, she only wanted to find her to blame her for the fire in the camp. Someone must have started it on purpose and with murderous intent—but that someone was not Alma!

I called Layla's name and ran after her with quick steps.

At that moment, I saw Alma stagger out of her tent. She had a blanket wrapped around her body, much like I had done myself.

"Go to her," I called to Layla, "and stay with her. Look for Optimus. I don't want him to let you out of his sight!"

Layla looked at me uncomprehendingly—but then she seemed to understand. No, she misunderstood me! I could see that in her eyes. She thought that I was instructing her to guard Alma.

Typical for Layla, that she believed me capable of giving her such an order! If I had thought Alma to be a ruthless killer, I would never have risked Layla's life by leaving them alone together.

"She is innocent," I called out to Layla—for which I only received another uncomprehending look. But there was no time for more extensive explanations now.

I gripped the hilt of my sword tighter and turned once in a circle to take in the situation in the camp.

No man was expendable here; I recognized that immediately. Every lad, every guard, even every slave girl was fighting the fire. They were carrying belongings, shoveling sand to prevent the flames from spreading—and in the meantime a veritable bucket brigade had formed that reached down to the lake.

I was on my own, but that didn't frighten me. I would find her and hunt her down, the madwoman who was responsible for all of this mayhem. *Zenobia*.

I plucked one of the oil lamps from the hook near the

campfire, or rather, near the inferno that had once been the campfire. I coughed, and sweat poured out of all my pores.

I turned away, left the camp behind me, and ran out into the desert. There I began to search the ground for tracks as quickly as possible, looking for telltale ones, which led out of the desert and towards our camp, or back in the opposite direction. The murderess must have come this way—and also have disappeared again, after her deed was done. After she had set the camp on fire, blinded by rage and revenge. The former unconditional love she had shown Alma must have turned into fierce hatred, since the beloved mistress had rejected her.

I walked in a large circle first around the left side of the camp, my eyes fixed on the ground, until I found myself near the lake shore. Then I directed my steps back in the opposite direction, again around the camp.

And finally I found what I was looking for: tracks in the sand left by someone who'd come in from the desert—and gone back there again. I followed them as fast as my legs would carry me.

I was not a trained tracker. The small lamp I had with me barely gave light, and the trail was already blurred by the wind that blew tonight. The perfect weather conditions if you wanted to start a fire that would spread quickly!

Strange noises followed me, dark shadows seemed to lie in wait wherever I turned. The desert might seem barren and empty during the day, but at night it came to life.

I had to think back to Lurco, who'd been finished off by the beasts of the desert after he'd been badly wounded. And to Optimus, who'd been attacked by a pride of lions.

Was I in for something similar if I ventured further into the darkness?

I gripped my sword tighter and quickened my steps. I was not a coward. I feared no predator. And also no murderer, however insidious! I knew that justice—and perhaps finally the will of the gods—was on my side.

The trail I was following broke off again and again, but I always managed to pick it up anew a few steps further on. Zenobia might have been familiar with poisonous animals, but she didn't know how to mislead a pursuer. She had marched towards the camp by the shortest route and returned after the deed was done, in an almost dead straight line, which was much too easy to follow.

Finally, I caught sight of a dark shadow that barely stood out from the night—but still unmistakably resembled a human figure. Only thirty or forty steps separated me from her. She had surely noticed me long ago and was now fleeing as fast as she could.

But not fast enough. Even though I was still coughing, still tasting the acrid stench of the fire, I struggled for breath and put my last strength into my legs.

Then finally I reached her. I let my hand shoot forward, got hold of her arm and yanked on it. It made her stumble. She fell to the ground, tried to crawl on all fours, but she didn't escape me. When I grabbed her again, she ducked and raised her arm protectively above her head.

But suddenly she smiled at me, seemingly relieved.

"Oh, it is you, sir!" she cried, "thank the gods. I thought the mistress had found me ... seeking my life!"

XXXV

Zenobia overwhelmed me with a mad flurry of words.

"The mistress is out of her mind," she wailed, "she has gone completely crazy!"

Then she went into a long litany of accusations: Alma had murdered her own husband and never wanted to belong to a man again. That's why she had killed Timotheos, whose advances had been repugnant to her—and had tried to do the same to me, because I'd also been courting her. And Lurco had found out about her misdeeds....

It was almost the same charge Layla had leveled against Alma. But Layla had been wrong!

Suddenly I realized how cleverly Zenobia had wrapped my former lover, my otherwise so-clever black Sphinx, around her finger. How she had sought Layla's friendship—with the sole purpose of whispering devious words to her about Alma! And she had indeed succeeded in deceiving Layla, a woman whose mind was as sharp as a blade of the best Celtic steel, and who knew how to solve even the most difficult riddles.

This time Layla had gone astray, deceived by a selfish and devious slave.

But I saw through Zenobia.

She talked to me incessantly. "I ran away because Alma wanted to kill me!" she cried. "I'd accused her of the murders, starting with her husband ... and suddenly she came at me, trying to get at my throat! I just managed to escape, running out into the desert. But I stayed around to warn you all. To warn you, in particular, sir! I know how you feel about her, but this woman brings death! I wanted to sneak into your tent tonight to reveal everything to you, but then I saw that the camp was on fire. She must have set the fire! Oh, she is possessed as if by a demon, I tell you!"

I had enough.

"Silence, you harpy!" I commanded the deceitful hag. "You don't fool me! It was *you* who committed all these acts. And why? Because you wanted Alma all to yourself? Because you are obsessed with her?"

"What, sir? No!"

"Oh please, enough of those lies! You took it upon yourself to free Alma from her tormentor. Alma's husband—you murdered him, because you were devoted to your mistress in loyal love. Far more than the love of a slave to her mistress, am I not right? You thought, once the master lay in his grave, a wonderful life would await you with Alma. In Rome together, just you and her. But Alma wanted to travel, wanted to see the world, which was anathema to you. From the beginning you tried to make her turn back, by pointing out every dark omen—and probably even staging some yourself. At first they were only signs, but Alma didn't want to see them. That's why you had to be more explicit, right? The roof tile in Rhodos? The date dish that you said made you sick, when it was meant for Alma? The chariot that almost ran over your mistress in Ephesus? How many of these alleged accidents or omens from the gods did you cause yourself, merely to frighten Alma into returning home? And then the tarantula in her chamber in Alexandria. You captured that animal, and you had no difficulty in smuggling it into Alma's room, knowing that the spider, though hideous, was harmless. At that time you didn't want to harm Alma—just to make her finally give up her journey. But your mistress is a brave woman, she did not do you the favor!"

I grabbed her roughly by the arm and shook her.

Zenobia began to sob, crying out again and again, "No, it's not true! You are doing me wrong, sir, I beseech you!"

But I was not finished yet.

"You realized," I continued in a sharp tone, "that nothing was to become of the tranquil life for two that you had envisioned, because Alma found pleasure in traveling—despite all the dark omens and dangers—and she also found pleasure in men! Being young, and a widow, she didn't want to be buried alive at home with a fearful slave. Timotheos's courtship flattered her, and—I dare to hope, anyway—mine much more so! But you did not want a new master, you wanted Alma for yourself. That's why you were after our lives, and also after the unfortunate Lurco, who must have been watching you and wanted to blackmail you. You wrapped yourself in Alma's distinctive cloak and came out of her tent when you went to the meeting with Timotheos, which you'd set up yourself by forging a letter from your mistress. And Lurco, walking around half asleep, as he was wont to do, may have mistaken you for your mistress in the cloak, with the hood on your head. Was it not so? Admit it! I know everything!"

This claim was a bit of an exaggeration—I had made up

the details of my accusation going along. But I knew that Zenobia was guilty. Or rather, my heart knew that Alma was innocent. So only her slave could be the murderer!

"In the end, you stopped at nothing," I continued breathlessly. "You devised a plan to set up your mistress as the murderer, insidiously but subtly casting suspicion on her. You stained her cloak with blood splatters when you attacked Timotheos ... yet you didn't bother to wash them out. And then, that night when Lurco was killed, you claimed—as if in passing—that Alma hadn't been in her tent when you went to check on her. Another lie to make her suspicious in our eyes! And of course, you yourself dropped Alma's fibula close to my tent on purpose, after you'd carried in that poisonous snake, all in the hope that Alma would flee when she was accused, and you two could finally return home. But Alma didn't do you that favor either. And when you finally realized that she was lost to you—when she dismissed you from her service because she could no longer bear your intrusive love—that's when you finally turned against her. Or rather against all of us. We all should become victims of the flames! But in our camp, there are some truly faithful slaves and guards, and at this very moment they are fighting the fire. A few possessions may be lost, but no one will lose his life. Except you, you snake! I would love to crucify you myself!"

At that moment, a blade flashed in Zenobia's hand. Just an instant ago she'd been a sobbing heap of misery and had protested her innocence, but now she showed her true colors. Like a fury, she leapt at me, trying to slash me with her blade.

With a courageous dive, I was just able to get myself out

of harm's way. Her blow went into the void. She, however, rushed at me again, wanting to strike once more....

But it did not come to that. My own arm, wielding the short sword, was faster and reached farther than hers. Zenobia jumped straight into the deadly blade.

Her hateful look broke, her body went limp. I rolled to the side, came to my knees, and looked at the wound I had inflicted on her.

She lay in the sand, bleeding, gasping—no longer to be saved for the world of the living.

Her last words were for Alma. "I gave everything for her!" she gasped through tears of anger—but still also of love? "I freed her from the tyrant, gave her my heart, my unbreakable loyalty. I protected and admired her ... and how did she repay me for all that? She trampled on her finally-won and so dearly paid freedom, wanting nothing more than a new oppressor! While I meant nothing to her."

She moaned in agony and pressed her hands into the pit of her stomach where my sword had wounded her. Blood flowed from her mouth.

"I am *not* an oppressor," I said to her.

Then Zenobia breathed her last.

XXXVI

The last Wonder of the World on our route, the famous statue of Zeus at Olympia, proved to be one of the most impressive.

Olympia itself may be familiar to every citizen of the Empire. The city—along with the sanctuary of Zeus—was founded by the legendary hero Hercules, who was the son of the god himself. And it was this brave fighter, too, who'd created the famous Games of Olympia, where the best athletes competed with each other in honor of the gods.

The statue of Zeus, however, the real Wonder of the World, was created centuries later—by Phidias, the most respected sculptor of his time. The cult image towered over forty feet high, up to the ceiling inside the temple, the dwelling place of the god, and for the Greeks it was the most sublime and glorious of all marvels.

Standing in front of the statue, I was inclined to agree with them. I felt as if the father of the gods himself was looking down on our heads.

The throne on which Zeus sat was crafted of ebony and ivory and lavishly set with gold and sparkling gems. Two golden Sphinxes served as armrests for Zeus, while two equally golden lions supported his footstool.

The eyes of the god, which looked down on us mortal worms so vividly and sublimely, were also made of glistening precious stone. His hair and beard were of gold and his skin of ivory.

In his open palms Zeus carried two more ornate sculptures. In the left a scepter on which a mighty eagle was enthroned, in the right a human-sized image of Nike, goddess of power and victory.

I had used the weeks of our return trip to Olympia to comfort Alma as much as possible and to cheer her up with my company. The fact that her own slave had three men on her conscience, and had almost killed us all in the end, was haunting her. At night I often heard her waking up screaming from terrible nightmares.

She always had her tent set up as close as possible to mine. Thus, whenever the terrible dream images tormented her, I could always rush over to hold her in my arms.

During the day, we talked about books, Wonders of the World, and all the destinations yet to be discovered in the future. *Together.* I invited her to return with us to Vindobona and be my guest for a while. Afterwards she could still decide whether to return to Rome or sell her property there. I hoped for the latter, of course, but I didn't want to push her.

Layla was horrified by her own failure. She admitted to Alma that she had seen in her the murderer, and did everything to make up for this guilt.

Alma did not bear her a grudge. "Zenobia deceived us all," she said bitterly.

The friendship between the two women, my favorite people in the world, blossomed anew. By the time we reached Olympia, we were already inseparable as a trio.

One evening when the two women had already gone to bed, Faustinius put his hand on my shoulder, as he was so fond of doing. "Well done, old friend," he said. "I almost want to say I envy you."

Of course, I also extended an invitation to Faustinius to come to Vindobona, and he promised that he would soon take me up on it. For the time being, however, he left us— together with his army of slaves and all the luxuries to which we had become so accustomed—halfway between Olympia and Vindobona. Urgent business led him to the western provinces of the Empire.

Another evening I had a conversation with Optimus in which I offered him a permanent position in my business.

I quoted an attractive salary and asked him to take over the management of my guard. He didn't hesitate for long, but accepted with pleasure.

Just a few days before we reached Vindobona, Layla wanted to talk to me. We were sitting across from each other in the refectory of a roadhouse where we had sought lodging for the night. Alma had already gone to bed.

"I've been thinking, Thanar," my former lover began. "Do you remember the conversation we had in Alexandria? We'd been wondering if we had incurred the wrath of the gods because they had already involved us in such terrible acts of blood on several occasions."

I nodded. "And now it has happened again," I said.

"That's true," Layla replied, "and this time I went completely astray—but you were able to solve the mystery, bringing the murderess to her just punishment. That means together we're ... well, very successful, aren't we?"

I had to laugh; Layla really was impossible. Once again our own lives had been at stake, yet she spoke about what had happened like a master craftsman who felt pride in his work. She really had an exceedingly strange inclination for murder and crime.

"I wonder," she continued, "if perhaps it is not the wrath of the gods that is afflicting us."

"But?" I asked incredulously.

"What if it's not a punishment—but a gift? A gift from the gods—the ability that together we are good at solving deadly mysteries, at unmasking murderers. Just think how often such crimes happen, and the victims' families are often left entirely to their own devices to track down the killer and bring him to justice. In most cases, they are hopelessly overburdened with this task. What the laws envisage—that the bereaved should go on a murder hunt in the midst of their grief—is hardly feasible. I don't know who came up with that idea. And possibly people would be putting themselves in danger in the process."

"And you'd rather put yourself in danger, right?" I countered, while silently admitting to myself that I did enjoy investigating crimes and solving murder mysteries with Layla.

And if I were completely honest: also putting myself in danger. At least in retrospect, when everything was over, it all no longer felt like a deadly threat, but more like a great and exciting adventure.

"So many murders go unpunished," Layla continued.

"We could help with that, I think."

"Yes ... and how?"

"I would like to invent, together with you, a ... well, a new profession for us. Your business is running without too much of your personal input by now, isn't it? And my days are filled with books, beautiful clothes, good food...."

And nights with Marcellus, I added in my mind.

"Not that I'm complaining," Layla continued quickly. "I'm very grateful for my life. But sometimes I get a wee bit bored in Marcellus's palace, if I'm honest. I want to do something useful, and I just think that we both, you and I, have a gift ... that the gods gave us and that we shouldn't let go to waste. We could actively offer our services when we learn of a crime, a murder. We could call ourselves, umm, *investigatores*. Or rather, *inquisitores*? *Detectores*? The latter sounds good, doesn't it? We enquire, investigate, and detect. And we bring criminals to justice."

I raised my cup of honey wine, which the innkeeper had just refilled for me, and toasted Layla. Of course, her suggestion was completely crazy. But who cared about that?

"*Detectores*, then," I said. "That really doesn't sound too bad."

Dramatis personae

Thanar: Germanic merchant with a weakness for Roman lifestyle and culture.
Layla: Thanar's freed slave and former lover, from the legendary kingdom of Nubia. Passionate sleuth and puzzle solver.
Titus Granius Marcellus: legate of the legionary camp of Vindobona. Layla's lover.

Alma Philonica: a young widow from Rome.
Zenobia: her body slave.

Gnaeus Saufeius Capito: a travel writer and hopeless talker.

Gaius Brutus Faustinius: an animal trader turned millionaire. An old friend of Thanar's.
Timotheos: scribe of Faustinius.
Lurco: barber of Faustinius.

Optimus: a former legionary. Thanar's guardsman.

More from Thanar and Layla:

THE DEADLY GLADIATRIX
Murder in Antiquity, Book 4

The inhabitants of the Roman provincial town of Vindobona are eagerly looking forward to great gladiatorial games. Among the fighters is a mysterious Amazon who can take on even the best of men. But why do the gladiatrix's opponents suddenly start dying as if struck down by the hand of the gods?

A tricky new case for Thanar and Layla, nosy amateur sleuths in Roman antiquity.

More from Alex Wagner:

If you enjoyed *Grand Tour into Death*, why not try my contemporary mystery series too?—*Penny Küfer Investigates*—cozy crime novels full of old world charm.

About the author

Alex Wagner lives with her husband and 'partner in crime' near Vienna, Austria. From her writing chair she has a view of an old ruined castle, which helps her to dream up the most devious murder plots.

Alex writes historical as well as contemporary murder mysteries, always trying to give you sleepless nights. ;)

You can learn more about her and her books on the internet and on Facebook:

www.alexwagner.at
www.facebook.com/AlexWagnerMysteryWriter